ROBERT SILVERBERG

BORN WITH THE DEAD

TOR

A TOM DOHERTY ASSOCIATES BOOK
NEW YORK

This is a work of fiction. All the characters and events portrayed in this book are fictitious, and any resemblance to real people or events is purely coincidental.

BORN WITH THE DEAD

Reprinted by permission of the author.

A TOR Book
Published by Tom Doherty Associates, Inc.
49 West 24 Street
New York, NY 10010

Cover art by Ron Walotsky

ISBN: 0-812-55952-5 Can. ISBN: 0-812-55953-3

Library of Congress Catalog Card Number: 88-50634

First edition: December 1988

Printed in the United States of America

0 9 8 7 6 5 4 3 2 1

THE TOR DOUBLES

Tor is proud to bring you the best in science fiction's short novels. An amazing amount of particularly fine science fiction is written at a length just too short to put in a book by itself, so we're providing them two at a time.

The Tor Doubles will be both new stories and older ones, all carefully chosen. Whichever side you start with, you will be able to turn the book over and enjoy the other side just as much.

THE DEAD LIVE DIFFERENTLY THAN WE DO

"She was traveling with four other deads, a woman and three men. Sharing her room with the archeologist, Zacharias. He acts as though he owns her. Perhaps he does. Do the deads marry? Is Zacharias her new husband?"

"It is very doubtful. The terms 'wife' and 'husband' are not in use among the deads. Instead they tend to create supportive pseudofamilial groupings of three or four or even more individuals, who—"

"Do you mean that all four of her companions in Zanzibar are her lovers?"

Jijibhoi gestured eloquently. "Who can say? I have reason to think that at certain times every dead may claim a familial relationship to all others of his kind. Who can say? We perceive the doings of the dead, as they say, through a glass, darkly."

Eventually Klein said, in a flat, toneless voice, "I have to get to see her."

Also by Robert Silverberg
published by Tor Books

ACROSS A BILLION YEARS
COLLISION COURSE
CONQUERORS FROM THE DARKNESS
INVADERS FROM EARTH
MASTER OF LIFE AND DEATH
NEXT STOP THE STARS
THE SILENT INVADERS
THE TIME OF THE GREAT FREEZE

1.

And what the dead had no speech for, when
living,
They can tell you, being dead: the commu-
nication
Of the dead is tongued with fire beyond the
language of the living.
T. S. Eliot: Little Gidding

Supposedly his late wife Sybille was on her way to Zanzibar. That was what they told him, and he believed it. Jorge Klein had reached that stage in his search when he would believe anything, if belief would only lead him to Sybille. Anyway, it wasn't so absurd that she would go to Zanzibar. Sybille had always wanted to go there. In some unfathomable obsessive way the place had seized the center of her consciousness long ago. When she was alive it hadn't been possible for her to go there, but now, loosed from all bonds, she would be drawn toward Zanzibar like a bird to its nest, like Ulysses to Ithaca, like a moth to a flame.

The plane, a small Air Zanzibar Havilland FP-803, took off more than half empty from Dar es

Salaam at 0915 on a mild bright morning, gaily circled above the dense masses of mango trees, red-flowering flamboyants, and tall coconut palms along the aquamarine shores of the Indian Ocean, and headed northward on the short hop across the strait to Zanzibar. This day—Tuesday, the ninth of March, 1993—would be an unusual one for Zanzibar: five deads were aboard the plane, the first of their kind ever to visit that fragrant isle. Daud Mahmoud Barwani, the health officer on duty that morning at Zanzibar's Karume Airport, had been warned of this by the emigration officials on the mainland. He had no idea how he was going to handle the situation, and he was apprehensive: these were tense times in Zanzibar. Times are always tense in Zanzibar. Should he refuse them entry? Did deads pose any threat to Zanzibar's ever-precarious political stability? What about subtler menaces? Deads might be carriers of dangerous spiritual maladies. Was there anything in the Revised Administrative Code about refusing visas on grounds of suspected contagions of the spirit? Daud Mahmoud Barwani nibbled moodily at his breakfast—a cold *chapatti,* a mound of cold curried potato—and waited without eagerness for the arrival of the deads.

Almost two and a half years had passed since Jorge Klein had last seen Sybille: the afternoon of Saturday, October 13, 1900, the day of her funeral. That day she lay in her casket as though merely asleep, her beauty altogether unmarred by her final ordeal: pale skin, dark lustrous hair, delicate nostrils, full lips. Iridescent gold and violet fabric enfolded her serene body; a shimmering electrostatic haze, faintly perfumed with a jasmine fragrance, protected her from decay. For five hours she floated on the dais while the rites of parting were read and the condolences were offered—offered almost furtively, as if her death were a thing too monstrous to acknowledge with a show of strong feeling; then, when only a few people remained, the inner core of their circle of friends, Klein kissed her lightly on the lips and surrendered her to the silent dark-clad men whom the Cold Town had sent. She had asked in her will to be rekindled; they took her away in a black van to work their magic on her corpse. The casket, retreating on their broad shoulders, seemed to Klein to be disappearing into a throbbing gray vortex that he was helpless to penetrate. Presumably he would never hear from her again. In those days the deads kept strictly to themselves, sequestered behind the walls of their self-imposed ghettos; it was rare ever to see one outside the Cold Towns, rare even for one of them to make oblique contact with the world of the living.

So a redefinition of their relationship was forced on him. For nine years it had been Jorge and Sybille, Sybille and Jorge, I and thou forming *we,* above all *we,* a transcendental *we.* He had loved her with almost painful intensity. In life they had gone everywhere together, had done everything together, shared research tasks and classroom assignments, thought interchangeable thoughts, expressed tastes that were nearly always identical, so completely had each permeated the other. She was a part of him, he of her, and until the moment of her unexpected death he had assumed it would be like that forever. They were still young, he 38, she 34, decades to look forward to. Then she was gone. And now they were mere anonymities to one another, she not Sybille but only a dead, he not Jorge but only a warm. She was somewhere on the North American continent, walking about, talking, eating, reading, and yet she was gone, lost to him, and it behooved him to accept that alteration in his life, and outwardly he did accept it, but yet, though he knew he could never again have things as they once had been, he allowed himself the indulgence of a lingering wistful hope of regaining her.

Shortly the plane was in view, dark against the brightness of the sky, a suspended mote, an irritating fleck in Barwani's eye, growing larger, causing him to blink and sneeze. Barwani was not ready for it. When Ameri Kombo, the flight controller in the cubicle next door, phoned him with the routine announcement of the landing, Barwani replied, "Notify the pilot that no one is to debark until I have given clearance. I must consult the regulations. There is possibly a peril to public health." For twenty minutes he let the plane sit, all hatches sealed, on the quiet runway. Wandering goats emerged from the shrubbery and inspected it. Barwani consulted no regulations. He finished his modest meal; then he folded his arms and sought to attain the proper state of tranquillity. These deads, he told himself, could do no harm. They were people like all other people, except that they had undergone extraordinary medical treatment. He must overcome his superstitious fear of them: he was no peasant, no silly clove-picker, nor was Zanzibar an abode of primitives. He would admit them, he would give them their anti-malaria tablets as though they were ordinary tourists, he would send them on their way. Very well. Now he was ready. He phoned Ameri Kombo. "There is no danger," he said. "The passengers may exit."

There were nine altogether, a sparse load. The four warms emerged first, looking somber and a little congealed, like people who had had to travel with a party of uncaged cobras. Barwani knew them all: the German consul's wife, the merchant Chowdhary's son, and two Chinese engineers, all returning from brief holidays in Dar. He waved them through the gate without formalities. Then came the deads, after an interval of half a minute: probably they had been sitting together at one end of the nearly empty plane and the others had been at the other. There were two women, three men, all of them tall and surprisingly robust-looking. He had expected them to shamble, to shuffle, to limp, to falter, but they moved with aggressive strides, as if they were in better health now than when they had been alive. When they reached the gate Barwani stepped forward to greet them, saying softly, "Health regulations, come this way, kindly." They were breathing, undoubtedly breathing: he tasted an emanation of liquor from the big red-haired man, a mysterious and pleasant sweet flavor, perhaps anise, from the dark-haired woman. It seemed to Barwani that their skins had an odd waxy texture, an unreal glossiness, but possibly that was his imagination; white skins had always looked artificial to him. The only certain difference he could detect about the deads was in their eyes, a way they had of remaining unnervingly fixed in a single intense gaze for many seconds before shifting. Those were the eyes, Barwani thought, of people who had looked upon the Emptiness without having been swallowed into it. A turbulence of questions erupted within him: What is it like, how do you feel, what do you remember, where did you go? He left them unspoken. Politely he said, "Welcome to the isle of cloves. We ask you to observe that malaria has been wholly eradicated here through extensive precautionary measures, and to prevent recurrence of unwanted disease we require of you that you take these tablets before proceeding further." Tourists often objected to that; these people swallowed their pills without a word of protest. Again Barwani yearned to reach toward them, to achieve some sort of contact that might perhaps help him to transcend the leaden weight of being. But an aura, a shield of strangeness, surrounded these five, and, though he was an amiable man who tended to fall into conversations easily with strangers, he passed them on in silence to Mponda the immigration man. Mponda's high forehead was shiny with sweat, and he chewed at his lower lip; evidently he was as disturbed by the deads as Barwani. He fumbled forms, he stamped a visa in the wrong place, he stammered while telling the deads that he must keep their passports overnight. "I shall post them by messenger to your hotel in the morning," Mponda promised them, and sent the visitors onward to the baggage pickup area with undue haste.

Klein had only one friend with whom he dared talk about it, a colleague of his at UCLA, a sleek little Parsee sociologist from Bombay named Framji Jijibhoi, who was as deep into the elaborate new subculture of the deads as a warm could get. "How can I accept this?" Klein demanded. "I can't accept it at all. She's out there somewhere, she's alive, she's—" Jijibhoi cut him off with a quick flick of his fingertips. "No, dear friend," he said sadly, "not alive, not alive at all, merely rekindled. You must learn to grasp the distinction." Klein could not learn to grasp the distinction. Klein could not learn to grasp anything having to do with Sybille's death. He could not bear to think that she had passed into another existence from which he was totally excluded. To find her, to speak with her, to participate in her experience of death and whatever lay beyond death, became his only purpose. He was inextricably bound to her, as though she were still his wife, as though Jorge-and-Sybille still existed in any way.

He waited for letters from her, but none came. After a few months he began trying to trace her, embarrassed by his own compulsiveness and by his increasingly open breaches of the etiquette of this sort of widowerhood. He traveled from one Cold Town to another—Sacramento, Boise, Ann Arbor, Louisville—but none would admit him, none would even answer his questions. Friends passed on rumors to him, that she was living among the deads of Tucson, of Roanoke, of Rochester, of San Diego, but nothing came of these tales; then Jijibhoi, who had tentacles into the world of the rekindled in many places, and who was aiding Klein in his quest even though he disapproved of its goal, brought him an authoritative-sounding report that she was at Zion Cold Town in southeastern Utah. They turned him away there too, but not entirely cruelly, for he did manage to secure plausible evidence that that was where Sybille really was.

In the summer of '92 Jijibhoi told him that Sybille had emerged from Cold Town seclusion. She had been seen, he said, in Newark, Ohio, touring the municipal golf course at Octagon State Memorial in the company of a swaggering red-haired archeologist named Kent Zacharias, also a dead, formerly a specialist in the mound-building Hopewellian cultures of the Ohio Valley. "It is a new phase," said Jijibhoi, "not unanticipated. The deads are beginning to abandon their early philosophy of total separatism. We have started to observe them as tourists visiting our world—exploring the life-death interface, as they like to term it. It will be very interesting, dear friend." Klein flew at once to Ohio and, without ever actually seeing her, tracked her from Newark to Chillicothe, from Chillicothe to Marietta, from Marietta into West Virginia, where he lost her trail somewhere between Moundsville and Wheeling. Two months later she was said to be in London, then in Cairo, then Addis Ababa. Early in '93 Klein learned, via the scholarly grapevine—an ex-Californian now at Nyerere University in

Arusha—that Sybille was on safari in Tanzania and was planning to go, in a few weeks, across to Zanzibar.

Of course. For ten years she had been working on a doctoral thesis on the establishment of the Arab Sultanate in Zanzibar in the early nineteenth century—studies unavoidably interrupted by other academic chores, by love affairs, by marriage, by financial reverses, by illnesses, death, and other responsibilities—and she had never actually been able to visit the island that was so central to her. Now she was free of all entanglements. Why shouldn't she go to Zanzibar at last? Why not? Of course: she was heading for Zanzibar. And so Klein would go to Zanzibar too, to wait for her.

As the five disappeared into taxis, something occurred to Barwani. He asked Mponda for the passports and scrutinized the names. Such strange ones: Kent Zacharias, Nerita Tracy, Sybille Klein, Anthony Gracchus, Laurence Mortimer. He had never grown accustomed to the names of Europeans. Without the photographs he would be unable to tell which were the women, which the men. Zacharias, Tracy, Klein . . . ah. *Klein.* He checked a memo, two weeks old, tacked to his desk. Klein, yes. Barwani telephoned the Shirazi Hotel—a project that consumed several minutes—and asked to speak with the American who had arrived ten days before, that slender man whose lips had been pressed tight in tension, whose eyes had glittered with fatigue, the one who had asked a little service of Barwani, a special favor, and had dashed him a much-needed hundred shillings as payment in advance. There was a lengthy delay, no doubt while porters searched the hotel, looking in the men's room, the bar, the lounge, the garden, and then the American was on the line. "The person about whom you inquired has just arrived, sir," Barwani told him.

2.

The dance begins. Worms underneath fingertips, lips beginning to pulse, heartache and throat-catch. All slightly out of step and out of key, each its own tempo and rhythm. Slowly, connections. Lip to lip, heart to heart, finding self in other, dreadfully, tentatively, burning . . . notes finding themselves in chords in sequence, cacophony turning to polyphonous contrapuntal chorus, a diapason of celebration.

R.D. Laing: The Bird of Paradise

Sybille stands timidly at the edge of the municipal golf course at Octagon State Memorial in Newark, Ohio, holding her sandals in her hand and surreptitiously working her toes into the lush, immaculate carpet of dense, close-cropped lime-green grass. It is a summer afternoon in 1992, very hot; the air, beautifully translucent, has that timeless midwestern shimmer, and the droplets of water from the morning sprinkling have not yet burned off the lawn. Such extraordinary grass! She hadn't often seen grass like that in California, and certainly not at Zion Cold Town in thirsty Utah. Kent Zacharias, towering beside her, shakes his head sadly. "A golf course!" he mutters. "One of the most important prehistoric sites in North America and they make a golf course out of it! Well, I suppose it could have been worse. They might have bulldozed the whole thing and turned it into a municipal parking lot. Look, there, do you see the earthworks?"

She is trembling. This is her first extended journey outside the Cold Town, her first venture into the world of the warms since her rekindling, and she is picking up threatening vibrations from all the life that burgeons about her. The park is surrounded by pleasant little houses, well kept. Children on bicycles rocket through the streets. In front of her, golfers are merrily slamming away. Little yellow golf carts clamber with lunatic energy over the rises and dips of the course. There are platoons of tourists who, like herself and Zacharias, have come to see the Indian mounds. There are dogs running free. All this seems menacing to her. Even the vegetation—the thick grass, the manicured shrubs, the heavy-leafed trees with low-hanging boughs—disturbs her. Nor is the nearness of Zacharias reassuring, for he too seems inflamed with undeadlike vitality; his face is florid, his gestures are broad and overanimated, as he points out the low flat-topped mounds, the grassy bumps and ridges making up the giant joined circle and octagon of the ancient monument. Of course, these mounds are the mainspring of his being, even now, five years post mortem. Ohio is his Zanzibar.

"—once covered four square miles. A grand ceremonial center, the Hopewellian equivalent of Chichen Itza, of Luxor, of—" He pauses. Awareness of her distress has finally filtered through the intensity of his archeological zeal. "How are you doing?" he asks gently.

She smiles a brave smile. Moistens her lips. Inclines her head toward the golfers, toward the tourists, toward the row of darling little houses outside the rim of the park. Shudders.

"Too cheery for you, is it?"

"Much," she says.

Cheery. Yes. A cheery little town, a magazine-cover town, a chamber-of-commerce town. Newark lies becalmed on the breast of the sea of time: but for the look of the automobiles, this could be 1980 or 1960 or perhaps 1940. Yes. Motherhood, baseball, apple pie, church every Sunday. Yes. Zacharias nods and makes one of the signs of comfort at her. "Come," he whispers. "Let's go toward the heart of the complex. We'll lose the twentieth century along the way."

With brutal imperial strides he plunges into the golf course. Long-legged Sybille must work hard to keep up with him. In a moment they are within the embankment, they have entered the sacred octagon, they have penetrated the vault of the past, and at once Sybille feels they have achieved a successful crossing of the interface between life and death. How still it is here! She senses the powerful presence of the forces of death, and those dark spirits heal her unease. The encroachments of the world of the living on these precincts of the dead become insignificant: the houses outside the park are no longer in view, the golfers are mere foolish incorporeal shadows, the bustling yellow golf carts become beetles, the wandering tourists are invisible.

She is overwhelmed by the size and symmetry of the ancient site. What spirits sleep here? Zacharias conjures them, waving his hands like a magician. She has heard so much from him already about these people, these Hopewellians—What did they call themselves? How can we ever know?—who heaped up these ramparts of earth twenty centuries ago. Now he brings them to life for her with gestures and low urgent words. He whispers fiercely:

—Do you see them?

And she does see them. Mists descend. The mounds reawaken; the mound-builders appear. Tall, slender, swarthy, nearly naked, clad in shining copper breastplates, in necklaces of flint disks, in bangles of bone and mica and tortoiseshell, in heavy chains of bright lumpy pearls, in rings of stone and terra-cotta, in armlets of bears' teeth and panthers' teeth, in spool-shaped metal ear ornaments, in furry loincloths. Here are priests in intricately woven robes and awesome masks. Here are chieftains with crowns of copper rods, moving in frosty dignity along the long earthen-walled avenue. The eyes of these people glow with energy. What an enormously vital, enormously profligate culture they sustain here! Yet Sybille is not alienated by their throbbing vigor, for it is the vigor of the dead, the vitality of the vanished.

Look, now. Their painted faces, their unblinking gazes. This is a funeral procession. The Indians have come to these intricate geometrical enclosures to perform their acts of worship, and now, solemnly parading along the perimeters of the circle and the octagon, they pass onward, toward the mortuary zone beyond. Zacharias and Sybille are left alone in the middle of the field. He murmurs to her:

—Come. We'll follow them.

He makes it real for her. Through his cunning craft she has access to this community of the dead. How easily she has drifted backward across time! She learns here that she can affix herself to the sealed past at any point; it's only the present, open-ended and unpredictable, that is troublesome. She and Zacharias float through the misty meadow, no sensation of feet touching ground; leaving the octagon, they travel now down a long grassy causeway to the place of the burial mounds, at the edge of a dark forest of wide-crowned oaks. They enter a vast clearing. In the center the ground has been plastered with clay, then covered lightly with sand and fine gravel; on this base the mortuary house, a roofless four-sided structure with walls consisting of rows of wooden palisades, has been erected. Within this is a low clay platform topped by a rectangular tomb of log cribbing, in which two bodies can be seen: a young man, a young woman, side by side, bodies fully extended, beautiful even in death. They wear copper breastplates, copper ear ornaments, copper bracelets, necklaces of gleaming yellowish bears' teeth.

Four priests station themselves at the corners of the mortuary house. The faces are covered by grotesque wooden masks topped by great antlers, and they carry wands two feet long, effigies of the death-cup mushroom in wood sheathed with copper. One priest commences a harsh, percussive chant. All four lift their wands and abruptly bring them down. It is a signal; the depositing of grave-goods begins. Lines of mourners bowed under, heavy sacks approach the mortuary house. They are unweeping, even joyful, faces ecstatic, eyes shining, for these people know what later cultures will forget, that death is no termination but rather a natural continuation of life. Their departed friends are to be envied. They are honored with lavish gifts, so that they may live like royalty in the next world: out of the sacks come nuggets of copper, meteoric iron, and silver, thousands of pearls, shell beads, beads of copper and iron, buttons of wood and stone, heaps of metal ear-spools, chunks and chips of obsidian, animal effigies carved from slate and bone and tortoiseshell, ceremonial copper axes and knives, scrolls cut from mica, human jawbones inlaid with turquoise, dark coarse pottery, needles of bone, sheets of woven cloth, coiled serpents fashioned from dark stone, a torrent of offerings, heaped up around and even upon the two bodies.

At length the tomb is choked with gifts. Again there is a signal from the priests. They elevate their wands and the mourners, drawing back to the borders of the clearing, form a circle and begin to sing a somber, throbbing funereal hymn. Zacharias, after a moment, sings with them, wordlessly embellishing the melody with heavy melismas. His voice is a rich *basso cantante,* so unexpectedly beautiful that Sybille is moved almost to confusion by it, and looks at him in awe. Abruptly he breaks off, turns to her, touches her arm, leans down to say:

—You sing too.

Sybille nods hesitantly. She joins the song, falteringly at first, her throat constricted by self-consciousness; then she finds herself becoming part of the rite, somehow, and her tone becomes more confident. Her high clear soprano soars brilliantly above the other voices.

Now another kind of offering is made: boys cover the mortuary house with heaps of kindling—twigs, dead branches, thick boughs, all sorts of combustible debris—until it is quite hidden from sight, and the priests cry a halt. Then, from the forest, comes a woman bearing a blazing firebrand, a girl, actually, entirely naked, her sleek fair-skinned body painted with bizarre horizontal stripes of red and green on breasts and buttocks and thighs, her long glossy black hair flowing like a cape behind her as she runs. Up to the mortuary house she sprints; breathlessly she touches the firebrand to the kindling, here, here, here, performing a wild dance as she goes, and hurls the torch into the center of the pyre. Skyward leap the flames in a ferocious rush. Sybille feels seared by the blast of heat. Swiftly the house and tomb are consumed.

While the embers still glow, the bringing of earth gets under way. Except for the priests, who remained rigid at the cardinal points of the site, and the girl who wielded the torch, who lies like discarded clothing at the edge of the clearing, the whole community takes part. There is an open pit behind a screen of nearby trees; the worshippers, forming lines, go to it and scoop up soil, carrying it to the burned mortuary house in baskets, in buckskin aprons, in big moist clods held in their bare hands. Silently they dump their burdens on the ashes and go back for more.

Sybille glances at Zacharias; he nods; they join the line. She goes down into the pit, gouges a lump of moist black clayey soil from its side, takes it to the growing mound. Back for another, back for another. The mound rises rapidly, two feet above ground level now, three, four, a swelling circular blister, its outlines governed by the unchanging positions of the four priests, its tapering contours formed by the tamping of scores of bare feet. Yes, Sybille thinks, this is a valid way of celebrating death, this is a fitting rite. Sweat runs down her body, her clothes become stained and muddy, and still she runs to the earth-quarry, runs from there to the mound, runs to the quarry, runs to the mound, runs, runs, transfigured, ecstatic.

Then the spell breaks. Something goes wrong, she does not know what, and the mists clear, the sun dazzles her eyes, the priests and the mound-builders and the unfinished mound disappear. She and Zacharias are once again in the octagon, golf carts roaring past them on every side. Three children and their parents stand just a few feet from her, staring, staring, and a boy about ten years old points to Sybille and says in a voice that reverberates through half of Ohio, "Dad, what's wrong with those people? Why do they look so weird?" Mother gasps and cries, "*Quiet,* Tommy, don't you have any manners?" Dad, looking furious, gives the boy a stinging blow across the face with the tips of his fingers, seizes him by the wrist, tugs him toward the other side of the park, the whole family following in their wake.

Sybille shivers convulsively. She turns away, clasping her hand to her betraying eyes. Zacharias embraces her. "It's all right," he says tenderly. "The boy didn't know any better. It's all right."

"Take me away from here!"

"I want to show you—"

"Some other time. Take me away. To the motel. I don't want to see anything. I don't want anybody to see me."

He takes her to the motel. For an hour she lies face down on the bed, racked by dry sobs. Several times she tells Zacharias she is unready for this tour, she wants to go back to the Cold Town, but he says nothing, simply strokes the tense muscles of her back, and after a while the mood passes. She turns to him and their eyes meet and he touches her and they make love in the fashion of the deads.

3.

> *Newness is renewal:* ad hoc enim venit, ut renovemur in illo; *making it new again, as on the first day;* herrlich wie am ersten Tag. *Reformation, or renaissance; rebirth. Life is Phoenix-like, always being born again out of its own death. The true nature of life is resurrection; all life is life after death, a second life, reincarnation.* Totus hic ordo revolubilis testatio est resurrectionis mortuorum. *The universal pattern of recurrence bears witness to the resurrection of the dead.*
>
> *Norman O. Brown:* Love's Body

"The rains shall be commencing shortly, gentleman and lady," the taxi driver said, speeding along the narrow highway to Zanzibar Town. He had been chattering steadily, wholly unafraid of his passengers. He must not know what we are, Sybille decided. "Perhaps in a week or two they begin. These shall be the long rains. The short rains come in the last of November and December."

"Yes, I know," Sybille said.

"Ah, you have been to Zanzibar before?"

"In a sense," she replied. In a sense she had been to Zanzibar many times, and how calmly she was taking it, now that the true Zanzibar was beginning to superimpose itself on the template in her mind, on that dream-Zanzibar she had carried about so long! She took everything calmly now; nothing excited her, nothing aroused her. In her former life the delay at the airport would have driven her into a fury: a ten-minute flight, and then to be trapped on the runway twice as long! But she had remained tranquil throughout it all, sitting almost immobile, listening vaguely to what Zacharias was saying and occasionally replying as if sending messages from some other planet. And now Zanzibar, so placidly accepted. In the old days she had felt a sort of paradoxical amazement whenever some landmark familiar from childhood geography lessons or the movies or travel posters—the Grand Canyon, the Manhattan skyline, Taos Pueblo—turned out in reality to look exactly as she imagined it would; but now here was Zanzibar, unfolding predictably and unsurprisingly before her, and she observed it with a camera's cool eye, unmoved, unresponsive.

The soft, steamy air was heavy with a burden of perfumes, not only the expected pungent scent of cloves but also creamier fragrances which perhaps were those of hibiscus, frangipani, jacaranda, bougainvillea, penetrating the cab's open window like probing tendrils. The imminence of the long rains was a tangible pressure, a presence, a heaviness in the atmosphere: at any moment a curtain might be drawn aside and the torrents would start. The highway was lined by two shaggy green walls of palms broken by tin-roofed shacks; behind the palms were mysterious dark groves, dense and alien. Along the edge of the road was the usual tropical array of obstacles: chickens, goats, naked children, old women with shrunken, toothless faces, all wandering around untroubled by the taxi's encroachment on their right-of-way. On through the rolling flatlands the cab sped, out onto the peninsula on which Zanzibar Town sits. The temperature seemed to be rising perceptibly minute by minute; a fist of humid heat was clamping tight over the island. "Here is the waterfront, gentleman and lady," the driver said. His voice was an intrusive hoarse purr, patronizing, disturbing. The sand was glaringly white, the water a dazzling glassy blue; a couple of dhows moved sleepily across the mouth of the harbor, their lateen sails bellying slightly as the gentle sea breeze caught them. "On this side, please—" An enormous white wooden building, four stories high, a wedding cake of long verandas and cast-iron railings, topped by a vast cupola. Sybille, recognizing it, anticipated the driver's spiel, hearing it like a subliminal pre-echo: "Beit al-Ajaib, the House of Wonders, former government house. Here the Sultan was often make great banquets, here the famous of all Africa came homaging. No longer in use. Next door the old Sultan's Palace, now Palace of People. You wish to go in House of Wonders? Is open: we stop, I take you now."

"Another time," Sybille said faintly. "We'll be here a while."

"You not here just a day like most?"

"No, a week or more. I've come to study the history of your island. I'll surely visit the Beit al-Ajaib. But not today."

"Not today, no. Very well: you call me, I take you anywhere. I am Ibuni." He gave her a gallant toothy grin over his shoulder and swung the cab inland with a ferocious lurch, into the labyrinth of winding streets and narrow alleys that was Stonetown, the ancient Arab quarter.

All was silent here. The massive white stone buildings presented blank faces to the streets. The windows, mere slits, were shuttered. Most doors—the famous paneled doors of Stonetown, richly carved, studded with brass, cunningly inlaid, each door an ornate Islamic masterpiece—were closed and seemed to be locked. The shops looked shabby, and the small display windows were speckled with dust. Most of the signs were so faded Sybille could barely make them out:

PREMCHAND'S EMPORIUM
MONJI'S CURIOS
ABDULLAH'S BROTHERHOOD STORE
MOTILAL'S BAZAAR

The Arabs were long since gone from Zanzibar. So were most of the Indians, though they were said to be creeping back. Occasionally, as it pursued its intricate course through the maze of Stonetown, the taxi passed elongated black limousines, probably of Russian or Chinese make, chauffeur-driven, occupied by dignified self-contained dark-skinned men in white robes. Legislators, so she supposed them to be, en route to meetings of state. There were no other vehicles in sight, and no pedestrians except for a few women, robed entirely in black, hurrying on solitary errands. Stonetown had none of the vitality of the countryside; it was a place of ghosts, she thought, a fitting place for vacationing deads. She glanced at Zacharias, who nodded and smiled, a quick quirky smile that acknowledged her perception and told her that he too had had it. Communication was swift among the deads and the obvious rarely needed voicing.

The route to the hotel seemed extraordinarily involuted, and the driver halted frequently in front of shops, saying hopefully, "You want brass chests, copper pots, silver curios, gold chains from China?" Though Sybille gently declined his suggestions, he continued to point out bazaars and emporiums, offering earnest recommendations of quality and moderate price, and gradually she realized, getting her bearings in the town, that they had passed certain corners more than once. Of course: the driver must be in the pay of shopkeepers who hired him to lure tourists. "Please take us to our hotel," Sybille said, and when he persisted in his huckstering—"Best ivory here, best lace"—she said it more firmly, but she kept her temper. Jorge would have been pleased by her transformation, she thought; he had all too often been the immediate victim of her fiery impatience. She did not know the specific cause of the change. Some metabolic side-effect of the rekindling process, maybe, or maybe her two years of communion with Guidefather at the Cold Town, or was it, perhaps, nothing more than the new knowledge that all of time was hers, that to let oneself feel hurried now was absurd?

"Your hotel is this," Ibuni said at last.

It was an old Arab mansion—high arches, innumerable balconies, musty air, electric fans turning sluggishly in the dark hallways. Sybille and Zacharias were given a sprawling suite on the third floor, overlooking a courtyard lush with palms, vermilion nandi, kapok trees, poinsettia, and agapanthus. Mortimer, Gracchus, and Nerita had long since arrived in the other cab and were in an identical suite one floor below. "I'll have a bath," Sybille told Zacharias. "Will you be in the bar?"

"Very likely. Or strolling in the garden."

He went out. Sybille quickly shed her travel-sweaty clothes. The bathroom was a Byzantine marvel, elaborate swirls of colored tile, an immense yellow tub standing high on bronze eagle-claw-and-globe legs. Lukewarm water dribbled in slowly when she turned the tap. She smiled at her reflection in the tall oval mirror. There had been a mirror somewhat like it at the rekindling house. On the morning after her awakening, five or six deads had come into her room to celebrate with her her successful transition across the interface, and they had had that big mirror with them; delicately, with great ceremoniousness, they had drawn the coverlet down to show herself to her in it, naked, slender, narrow-waisted, high-breasted, the beauty of her body unchanged, marred neither by dying nor by rekindling, indeed enhanced by it, so that she had become more youthful-looking and even radiant in her passage across that terrible gulf.

—You're a very beautiful woman.

That was Pablo. She would learn his name and all the other names later.

—I feel such a flood of relief. I was afraid I'd wake up and find myself a shriveled ruin.

—That could not have happened, Pablo said.

—And never will happen, said a young woman. Nerita, she was.

—But deads do age, don't they?

—Oh, yes, we age, just as the warms do. But not *just* as.

—More slowly?

—Very much more slowly. And differently. All our biological processes operate more slowly, except the functions of the brain, which tend to be quicker than they were in life.

—Quicker?

—You'll see.

—It all sounds ideal.

—We are extremely fortunate. Life has been kind to us. Our situation is, yes, ideal. We are the new aristocracy.

—The new aristocracy—

Sybille slipped slowly into the tub, leaning back against the cool porcelain, wriggling a little, letting the tepid water slide up as far as her throat. She closed her eyes and drifted peacefully. All of Zanzibar was waiting for her. *Streets I never thought I should visit.* Let Zanzibar wait. Let Zanzibar wait. *Words I never thought to speak. When I left my body on a distant shore.* Time for everything, everything in its due time.

—*You're a very beautiful woman,* Pablo had told her, not meaning to flatter.

Yes. She had wanted to explain to them, that first morning, that she didn't really care all that much about the appearance of her body, that her real priorities lay elsewhere, were "higher," but there hadn't been any need to tell them that. They understood. They understood everything. Besides, she *did* care about her body. Being beautiful was less important to her than it was to those women for whom physical beauty was their only natural advantage, but her appearance mattered to her; her body pleased her and she knew it was pleasing to others, it gave her access to people, it was a means of making connections, and she had always been grateful for that. In her other existence her delight in her body had been flawed by the awareness of the inevitability of its slow steady decay, the certainty of the loss of that accidental power that beauty gave her, but now she had been granted exemption from that: she would change with time but she would not have to feel as warms must feel, that she was gradually falling apart. Her rekindled body would not betray her by turning ugly. No.

—*We are the new aristocracy*

After her bath she stood a few minutes by the open window, naked to the humid breeze. Sounds came to her: distant bells, the bright chatter of tropical birds, the voices of children singing in a language she could not identify. Zanzibar! Sultans and spices, Livingstone and Stanley, Tippu Tib the slaver, Sir Richard Burton spending a night in this very hotel room, perhaps. There was a dryness in her throat, a throbbing in her chest: a little excitement coming alive in her after all. She felt anticipation, even eagerness. All Zanzibar lay before her. Very well. Get moving, Sybille, put some clothes on, let's have lunch, a look at the town.

She took a light blouse and shorts from her suitcase. Just then Zacharias returned to the room, and she said, not looking up, "Kent, do you think it's all right for me to wear these shorts here? They're—" A glance at his face and her voice trailed off. "What's wrong?"

"I've just been talking to your husband."

"He's *here?*"

"He came up to me in the lobby. Knew my name. 'You're Zacharias,' he said, with a Bogarty little edge to his voice, like a deceived movie husband confronting the Other Man. 'Where is she? I have to see her.' "

"Oh, no, Kent."

"I asked him what he wanted with you. 'I'm her husband,' he said, and I told him, 'Maybe you were her husband once, but things have changed,' and then—"

"I can't imagine Jorge talking tough. He's such a *gentle* man, Kent! How did he look?"

"Schizoid," Zacharias said. "Glassy eyes, muscles bunching in his jaws, signs of terrific pressure all over him. He knows he's not supposed to do things like this, doesn't he?"

"Jorge knows exactly how he's supposed to behave. Oh, Kent, what a stupid mess! Where is he now?"

"Still downstairs. Nerita and Laurence are talking to him. You don't want to see him, do you?"

"Of course not."

"Write him a note to that effect and I'll take it down to him. Tell him to clear off."

Sybille shook her head. "I don't want to hurt him."

"Hurt him? He's followed you halfway around the world like a lovesick boy, he's tried to violate your privacy, he's disrupted an important trip, he's refused to abide by the conventions that govern the relationships of warms and deads, and you—"

"He loves me, Kent."

"He loved you. All right, I concede that. But the person he loved doesn't exist any more. He has to be made to realize that."

Sybille closed her eyes. "I don't want to hurt him. I don't want you to hurt him either."

"I won't hurt him. Are you going to see him?"

"No," she said. She grunted in annoyance and threw her shorts and blouse into a chair. There was a fierce pounding at her temples, a sensation of being challenged, of being threatened, that she had not felt since that awful day at the Newark mounds. She strode to the window and looked out, half expecting to see Jorge arguing with Nerita and Laurence in the courtyard. But there was no one down there except a houseboy who looked up as if her bare breasts were beacons and gave her a broad dazzling smile. Sybille turned her back to him and said dully, "Go back down. Tell him that it's impossible for me to see him. Use that word. Not that I *won't* see him, not that I *don't want* to see him, not that it isn't *right* for me to see him, just that it's impossible. And then phone the airport. I want to go back to Dar on the evening plane."

"But we've only just arrived!"

"No matter. We'll come back some other time. Jorge is very persistent; he won't accept anything but a brutal rebuff, and I can't do that to him. So we'll leave."

Klein had never seen deads at close range before. Cautiously, uneasily, he stole quick intense looks at Kent Zacharias as they sat side by side on rattan chairs among the potted palms in the lobby of the hotel. Jijibhoi had told him that it hardly showed, that you perceived it more subliminally than by any outward manifestation, and that was true; there was a certain look about the eyes, of course, the famous fixity of the deads, and there was something oddly pallid about Zacharias' skin *beneath* the florid complexion, but if Klein had not known what Zacharias was he might not have guessed it. He tried to imagine this man, this red-haired red-faced dead archeologist, this digger of dirt mounds, in bed with Sybille. Doing with her whatever it was that the deads did in their couplings. Even Jijibhoi wasn't sure. Something with hands, with eyes, with whispers and smiles, not at all genital—so Jijibhoi believed. *This is Sybille's lover I'm talking to. This is Sybille's lover.* How strange that it bothered him so. She had had affairs when she was living; so had he; so had everyone; it was the way of life. But he felt threatened, overwhelmed, defeated, by this walking corpse of a lover.

Klein said, "Impossible?"

"That was the word she used."

"Can't I have ten minutes with her?"

"Impossible."

"Would she let me see her for a few moments, at least? I'd just like to find out how she looks."

"Don't you find it humiliating, doing all this scratching around just for a glimpse of her?"

"Yes."

"And you still want it?"

"Yes."

Zacharias sighed. "There's nothing I can do for you. I'm sorry."

"Perhaps Sybille is tired from having done so much traveling. Do you think she might be in a more receptive mood tomorrow?"

"Maybe," Zacharias said. "Why don't you come back then?"

"You've been very kind."

"De nada."

"Can I buy you a drink?"

"Thanks, no," Zacharias said. "I don't indulge any more. Not since—" He smiled.

Klein could smell whiskey on Zacharias' breath. All right, though. All right. He would go away. A driver waiting outside the hotel grounds poked his head out of his cab window and said hopefully, "Tour of the island, gentleman? See the clove plantations, see the athlete stadium?"

"I've seen them already," Klein said. He shrugged. "Take me to the beach."

He spent the afternoon watching turquoise wavelets lapping pink sand. The next morning he returned to Sybille's hotel, but they were gone, all five of them, gone on last night's flight to Dar, said the apologetic desk clerk. Klein asked if he could make a telephone call, and the clerk showed him an ancient instrument in an alcove near the bar. He phoned Barwani. "What's going on?" he demanded. "You told me they'd be staying at least a week!"

"Oh, sir, things change," Barwani said softly.

4.

What portends? What will the future bring? I do not know, I have no presentiment. When a spider hurls itself down from some fixed point, consistently with its nature, it always sees before it only an empty space wherein it can find no foothold however much it sprawls. And so it is with me: always before me an empty space; what drives me forward is a consistency which lies behind me. This life is topsy-turvy and terrible, not to be endured.

Søren Kierkegaard: Either/Or

Jijibhoi said, "In the entire question of death who is to say what is right, dear friend? When I was a boy in Bombay it was not unusual for our Hindu neighbors to practice the rite of suttee, that is, the burning of the widow on her husband's funeral pyre, and by what presumption may we call them barbarians? Of course"—his dark eyes flashed mischievously—"we *did* call them barbarians, though never when they might hear us. Will you have more curry?"

Klein repressed a sigh. He was getting full, and the curry was fiery stuff, of an incandescence far beyond his usual level of tolerance; but Jijibhoi's hospitality, unobtrusively insistent, had a certain hieratic quality about it that made Klein feel like a blasphemer whenever he refused anything in his home. He smiled and nodded, and Jijibhoi, rising, spooned a mound of rice into Klein's plate, buried it under curried lamb, bedecked it with chutneys and sambals. Silently, unbidden, Jijibhoi's wife went to the kitchen and returned with a cold bottle of Heineken's. She gave Klein a shy grin as she set it down before him. They worked well together, these two Parsees, his hosts.

They were an elegant couple—striking, even. Jijibhoi was a tall, erect man with a forceful aquiline nose, dark Levantine skin, jet black hair, a formidable mustache. His hands and feet were extraordinarily small; his manner was polite and reserved; he moved with a quickness of action bordering on nervousness. Klein guessed that he was in his early forties, though he suspected his estimate could easily be off by ten years in either direction. His wife—strangely, Klein had never been told her name—was younger than her husband, nearly as tall, fair of complexion—a light olive tone—and voluptuous of figure. She dressed invariably in flowing silken saris; Jijibhoi affected western business dress, suits and ties in styles twenty years out of date. Klein had never seen either of them bareheaded: she wore a kerchief of white linen, he a brocaded skullcap that might lead people to mistake him for an Oriental Jew. They were childless and self-sufficient, forming a closed dyad, a perfect unit, two segments of the same entity, conjoined and indivisible, as Klein and Sybille once had been. Their harmonious interplay of thought and gesture made them a trifle disconcerting, even intimidating, to others. As Klein and Sybille once had been.

Klein said, "Among your people—"

"Oh, very different, very different, quite unique. You know of our funeral custom?"

"Exposure of the dead, isn't it?"

Jijibhoi's wife giggled. "A very ancient recycling scheme!"

"The Towers of Silence," Jijibhoi said. He went to the dining room's vast window and stood with his back to Klein, staring out at the dazzling lights of Los Angeles. The Jijibhois' house, all redwood and glass, perched precariously on stilts near the crest of Benedict Canyon, just below Mulholland: the view took in everything from Hollywood to Santa Monica. "There are five of them in Bombay," said Jijibhoi, "on Malabar Hill, a rocky ridge overlooking the Arabian Sea. They are centuries old, each one circular, several hundred feet in circumference, surrounded by a stone wall twenty or thirty feet high. When a Parsee dies—do you know of this?"

"Not as much as I'd like to know."

"When a Parsee dies, he is carried to the Towers on an iron bier by professional corpse-bearers; the mourners follow in procession, two by two, joined hand to hand by holding a white handkerchief between them. A beautiful scene, dear Jorge. There is a doorway in the stone wall through which the corpse-bearers pass, carrying their burden. No one else may enter the Tower. Within is a circular platform paved with large stone slabs and divided into three rows of shallow, open receptacles. The outer row is used for the bodies of males, the next for those of females, the innermost one for children. The dead one is given a resting-place; vultures rise from the lofty palms in the gardens adjoining the Towers; within an hour or two, only bones remain. Later, the bare, sun-dried skeleton is cast into a pit at the center of the Tower. Rich and poor crumble together there into dust."

"And all Parsees are—ah—buried in this way?"

"Oh, no, no, by no means," Jijibhoi said heartily. "All ancient traditions are in disrepair nowadays, do you not know? Our younger people advocate cremation or even conventional interment. Still, many of us continue to see the beauty of our way."

"—beauty?—"

Jijibhoi's wife said in a quiet voice, "To bury the dead in the ground, in a moist tropical land where diseases are highly contagious, seems not sanitary to us. And to burn a body is to waste its substance. But to give the bodies of the dead to the efficient hungry birds—quickly, cleanly, without fuss—is to us a way of celebrating the economy of nature. To have one's bones mingle in the pit with the bones of the entire community is, to us, the ultimate democracy."

"And the vultures spread no contagions themselves, feeding as they do on the bodies of—"

"Never," said Jijibhoi firmly. "Nor do they contract our ills."

"And I gather that you both intend to have your bodies returned to Bombay when you—" Aghast, Klein paused, shook his head, coughed in embarrassment, forced a weak smile. "You see what this radioactive curry of yours has done to my manners? Forgive me. Here I sit, a guest at your dinner table, quizzing you about your funeral plans!"

Jijibhoi chuckled. "Death is not frightening to us, dear friend. It is—one hardly needs say it, does one?—it is a natural event. For a time we are here, and then we go. When our time ends, yes, she and I will give ourselves to the Towers of Silence."

His wife added sharply, "Better there than the Cold Towns! Much better!"

Klein had never observed such vehemence in her before.

Jijibhoi swung back from the window and glared at her. Klein had never seen that before either. It seemed as if the fragile web of elaborate courtesy that he and these two had been spinning all evening was suddenly unraveling, and that even the bonds between Jijibhoi and his wife were undergoing strain. Agitated now, fluttery, Jijibhoi began to collect the empty dishes, and after a long awkward moment said, "She did not mean to give offense."

"Why should I be offended?"

"A person you love chose to go to the Cold Towns. You might think there was implied criticism of her in my wife's expression of distaste for—"

Klein shrugged. "She's entitled to her feelings about rekindling. I wonder, though—"

He halted, uneasy, fearing to probe too deeply.

"Yes?"

"It was irrelevant."

"Please," Jijibhoi said. "We are old friends."

"I was wondering," said Klein slowly, "if it doesn't make things hard for you, spending all your time among deads, studying them, mastering their ways, devoting your whole career to them, when your wife evidently despises the Cold Towns and everything that goes on in them. If the theme of your work repels her you must not be able to share it with her."

"Oh," Jijibhoi said, tension visibly going from him, "if it comes to that, I have even less liking for the entire rekindling phenomenon than she."

"You do?" This was a side of Jijibhoi that Klein had never suspected. "It repels you? Then why did you choose to make such an intensive survey of it?"

Jijibhoi looked genuinely amazed. "What? Are you saying one must have personal allegiance to the subject of one's field of scholarship?" He laughed. "You are of Jewish birth, I think, and yet your doctoral thesis was concerned, was it not, with the early phases of the Third Reich?"

Klein winced. "Touché!"

"I find the subculture of the deads irresistible, as a

sociologist," Jijibhoi went on. "To have such a radical new aspect of human existence erupt during one's career is an incredible gift. There is no more fertile field for me to investigate. Yet I have no wish, none at all, ever to deliver myself up for rekindling. For me, for my wife, it will be the Towers of Silence, the hot sun, the obliging vultures—and finish, the end, no more, terminus."

"I had no idea you felt this way. I suppose if I'd known more about Parsee theology, I might have realized—"

"You misunderstand. Our objections are not theological. It is that we share a wish, an idiosyncratic whim, not to continue beyond the allotted time. But also I have serious reservations about the impact of rekindling on our society. I feel a profound distress at the presence among us of these deads, I feel a purely private fear of these people and the culture they are creating, I feel even an abhorrence for—" Jijibhoi cut himself short. "Your pardon. That was perhaps too strong a word. You see how complex my attitudes are toward this subject, my mixture of fascination and repulsion? I exist in constant tension between those poles. But why do I tell you all this, which if it does not disturb you must surely bore you? Let us hear about your journey to Zanzibar."

"What can I say? I went, I waited a couple of weeks for her to show up, I wasn't able to get near her at all, and I came home. All the way to Africa and I never even had a glimpse of her."

"What a frustration, dear Jorge!"

"She stayed in her hotel room. They wouldn't let me go upstairs to her."

"They?"

"Her entourage," Klein said. "She was traveling with four other deads, a woman and three men. Sharing her room with the archeologist, Zacharias. He was the one who shielded her from me, and did it very cleverly, too. He acts as though he owns her. Perhaps he does. What can you tell me, Framji? Do the deads marry? Is Zacharias her new husband?"

"It is very doubtful. The terms 'wife' and 'husband' are not in use among the deads. They form relationships, yes, but pair-bonding seems to be uncommon among them, possibly altogether unknown. Instead they tend to create supportive pseudo-familial groupings of three or four or even more individuals, who—"

"Do you mean that all four of her companions in Zanzibar are her lovers?"

Jijibhoi gestured eloquently. "Who can say? If you mean in a physical sense, I doubt it, but one can never be sure. Zacharias seems to be her special companion, at any rate. Several of the others may be part of her pseudo-family also, or all, or none. I have reason to think that at certain times every dead may claim a familial relationship to all others of his kind. Who can say? We perceive the doings of these people, as they say, through a glass, darkly."

"I don't see Sybille even that well. I don't even know what she looks like now."

"She has lost none of her beauty."

"So you've told me before. But I want to see her myself. You can't really comprehend, Framji, how much I want to see her. The pain I feel, not able—"

"Would you like to see her right now?"

Klein shook in a convulsion of amazement. "What? What do you mean? Is she—"

"Hiding in the next room? No, no, nothing like that. But I do have a small surprise for you. Come into the library." Smiling expansively, Jijibhoi led the way from the dining room to the small study adjoining it, a room densely packed from floor to ceiling with books in an astonishing range of languages—not merely English, French, and German, but also Sanskrit, Hindi, Gujarati, Farsi, the tongues of Jijibhoi's polyglot upbringing among the tiny Parsee colony of Bombay, a community in which no language once cherished was ever discarded. Pushing aside a stack of dog-eared professional journals, he drew forth a glistening picture-cube, activated its inner light with a touch of his thumb, and handed it to Klein.

The sharp, dazzling holographic image showed three figures in a broad grassy plain that seemed to have no limits and was without trees, boulders, or other visual interruptions, an endlessly unrolling green carpet under a blank death-blue sky. Zacharias stood at the left, his face averted from the camera; he was looking down, tinkering with the action of an enormous rifle. At the far right stood a stocky, powerful-looking dark-haired man whose pale, harsh-featured face seemed all beard and nostrils. Klein recognized him: Anthony Gracchus, one of the deads who had accompanied Sybille to Zanzibar. Sybille stood beside him, clad in khaki slacks and a crisp white blouse. Gracchus' arm was extended; evidently he had just pointed out a target to her, and she was intently aiming a gun nearly as big as Zacharias'.

Klein shifted the cube about, studying her face from various angles, and the sight of her made his fingers grow thick and clumsy, his eyelids to quiver. Jijibhoi had spoken truly: she had lost none of her beauty. Yet she was not at all the Sybille he had known. When he had last seen her, lying in her casket, she had seemed to be a flawless marble image of herself, and she had that same surreal statuary appearance now. Her face was an expressionless mask, calm, remote, aloof; her eyes were glossy mysteries; her lips registered a faint, enigmatic, barely perceptible smile. It frightened him to behold her this way, so alien, so unfamiliar. Perhaps it was the intensity of her concentration that gave her that forbidding marmoreal look, for she seemed to be pouring her entire being into the task of taking aim. By tilting the cube more extremely, Klein was able to see what she was aiming at: a strange awkward bird moving through the grass at the lower left, a bird larger than a turkey, round as a sack, with ash-gray plumage, a whitish breast and tail, yellow-white wings, and short, comical yellow legs. Its head was immense and its black bill ended in a great snubbed hook. The creature seemed solemn, rather dignified, and faintly absurd; it showed no awareness that its doom was upon it. How odd that Sybille should be about to kill it, she who had always detested the taking of life: Sybille the huntress now, Sybille the lunar goddess, Sybille-Diana!

Shaken, Klein looked up at Jijibhoi and said, "Where was this taken? On that safari in Tanzania, I suppose."

"Yes. In February. This man is the guide, the white hunter."

"I saw him in Zanzibar. Gracchus, his name is. He was one of the deads traveling with Sybille."

"He operates a hunting preserve not far from Kilimanjaro," Jijibhoi said, "that is set aside exclusively for the use of the deads. One of the more bizarre manifestations of their subculture, actually. They hunt only those animals which—"

Klein said impatiently, "How did you get this picture?"

"It was taken by Nerita Tracy, who is one of your wife's companions."

"I met her in Zanzibar too. But how—"

"A friend of hers is an acquaintance of mine, one of my informants, in fact, a valuable connection in my researches. Some months ago I asked him if he could obtain something like this for me. I did not tell him, of course, that I meant it for you." Jijibhoi looked close. "You seem troubled, dear friend."

Klein nodded. He shut his eyes as though to protect them from the glaring surfaces of Sybille's photograph. Eventually he said in a flat, toneless voice, "I have to get to see her."

"Perhaps it would be better for you if you would abandon—"

"No."

"Is there no way I can convince you that it is dangerous for you to pursue your fantasy of—"

"No," Klein said. "Don't even try. It's necessary for me to reach her. Necessary."

"How will you accomplish this, then?"

Klein said mechanically, "By going to Zion Cold Town."

"You have already done that. They would not admit you."

"This time they will. They don't turn away deads."

The Parsee's eyes widened. "You will surrender your own life? Is this your plan? What are you saying, Jorge?"

Klein, laughing, said, "That isn't what I meant at all."

"I am bewildered."

"I intend to infiltrate. I'll disguise myself as one of them. I'll slip into the Cold Town the way an infidel slips into Mecca." He seized Jijibhoi's wrist. "Can you help me? Coach me in their ways, teach me their jargon?"

"They'll find you out instantly."

"Maybe not. Maybe I'll get to Sybille before they do."

"This is insanity," Jijibhoi said quietly.

"Nevertheless. You have the knowledge. Will you help me?"

Gently Jijibhoi withdrew his arm from Klein's grasp. He crossed the room and busied himself with an untidy bookshelf for some moments, fussily arranging and rearranging. At length he said, "There is little I can do for you myself. My knowledge is broad but not deep, not deep enough. But if you insist on going through with this, Jorge, I can introduce you to someone who may be able to assist you. He is one of my informants, a dead, a man who has rejected the authority of the Guidefathers, a person who is *of* the deads but not *with* them. Possibly he can instruct you in what you would need to know."

"Call him," Klein said.

"I must warn you he is unpredictable, turbulent, perhaps even treacherous. Ordinary human values are without meaning to him in his present state."

"Call him."

"If only I could discourage you from—"

"Call him."

5.

> *Quarreling brings trouble. These days lions roar a great deal. Joy follows grief. It is not good to beat children much. You had better go away now and go home. It is impossible to work today. You should go to school every day. It is not advisable to follow this path, there is water in the way. Never mind, I shall be able to pass. We had better go back quickly. These lamps use a lot of oil. There are no mosquitoes in Nairobi. There are no lions here. There are people here, looking for eggs. Is there water in the well? No, there is none. If there are only three people, work will be impossible today.*
>
> *D. V. Perrott:* Teach Yourself Swahili

Gracchus signals furiously to the porters and bellows, *"Shika njia hii hii!"* Three turn, two keep trudging along. *"Ninyi nyote!"* he calls. *"Fanga kama hivi!"* He shakes his head, spits, flicks sweat from his forehead. He adds, speaking in a lower voice and in English, taking care that they will not hear him,

"Do as I say, you malevolent black bastards, or you'll be deader than I am before sunset!"

Sybille laughs nervously. "Do you always talk to them like that?"

"I try to be easy on them. But what good does it do, what good does any of it do? Come on, let's keep up with them."

It is less than an hour after dawn but already the sun is very hot, here in the flat dry country between Kilimanjaro and Serengeti. Gracchus is leading the party northward across the high grass, following the spoor of what he thinks is a quagga, but breaking a trail in the high grass is hard work and the porters keep veering away toward a ravine that offers the tempting shade of a thicket of thorn trees, and he constantly has to harass them in order to hold them to the route he wants. Sybille has noticed that Gracchus shouts fiercely to his blacks, as if they were no more than recalcitrant beasts, and speaks of them behind their backs with a rough contempt, but it all seems done for show, all part of his white-hunter role: she has also noticed, at times when she was not supposed to notice, that privately Gracchus is in fact gentle, tender, even loving among the porters, teasing them—she supposes—with affectionate Swahili banter and playful mock-punches. The porters are role-players too: they behave in the traditional manner of their profession, alternately deferential and patronizing to the clients, alternately posing as all-knowing repositories of the lore of the bush and as simple, guileless savages fit only for carrying burdens. But the clients they serve are not quite like the sportsmen of Hemingway's time, since they are deads, and secretly the porters are terrified of the strange beings whom they serve. Sybille has seen them muttering prayers and fondling amulets whenever they accidentally touch one of the deads, and has occasionally detected an unguarded glance conveying unalloyed fear, possibly revulsion. Gracchus is no friend of theirs, however jolly he may get with them: they appear to regard him as some sort of monstrous sorcerer and the clients as fiends made manifest.

Sweating, saying little, the hunters move in single file, first the porters with the guns and supplies, then Gracchus, Zacharias, Sybille, Nerita constantly clicking her camera, and Mortimer. Patches of white cloud drift slowly across the immense arch of the sky. The grass is lush and thick, for the short rains were unusually heavy in December. Small animals scurry through it, visible only in quick flashes, squirrels and jackals and guinea-fowl. Now and then larger creatures can be seen: three haughty ostriches, a pair of snuffling hyenas, a band of Thomson gazelles flowing like a tawny river across the plain. Yesterday Sybille spied two warthogs, some giraffes, and a serval, an elegant big-eared wildcat, that slithered along like a miniature cheetah. None of these beasts may be hunted, but only those special ones that the operators of the preserve have introduced for the special needs of their clients; anything considered native African wildlife, which is to say anything that was living here before the deads leased this tract from the Masai, is protected by government decree. The Masai themselves are allowed to do some lion-hunting, since this is their reservation, but there are so few Masai left that they can do little harm. Yesterday, after the warthogs and before the giraffes, Sybille saw her first Masai, five lean, handsome, long-bodied men, naked under skimpy red robes, drifting silently through the bush, pausing frequently to stand thoughtfully on one leg, propped against their spears. At close range they were less handsome—toothless, fly-specked, herniated. They offered to sell their spears and their beaded collars for a few shillings, but the safarigoers had already stocked up on Masai artifacts in Nairobi's curio shops, at astonishingly higher prices.

All through the morning they stalk the quagga, Gracchus pointing out hoofprints here, fresh dung there. It is Zacharias who has asked to shoot a quagga. "How can you tell we're not following a zebra?" he asks peevishly.

Gracchus winks. "Trust me. We'll find zebras up ahead too. But you'll get your quagga. I guarantee it."

Ngiri, the head porter, turns and grins. "*Piga quagga m'uzuri, bwana*," he says to Zacharias, and winks also, and then—Sybille sees it plainly—his jovial confident smile fades as though he has had the courage to sustain it only for an instant, and a veil of dread covers his dark glossy face.

"What did he say?" Zacharias asks.

"That you'll shoot a fine quagga," Gracchus replies.

Quaggas. The last wild one was killed about 1870, leaving only three in the world, all females, in European zoos. The Boers had hunted them to the edge of extinction in order to feed their tender meat to Hottentot slaves and to make from their striped hides sacks for Boer grain, leather *veldschoen* for Boer feet. The quagga of the London zoo died in 1872, that in Berlin in 1875, the Amsterdam quagga in 1883, and none was seen alive again until the artificial revival of the species through breedback selection and genetic manipulation in 1990, when this hunting preserve was opened to a limited and special clientele.

It is nearly noon, now, and not a shot has been fired all morning. The animals have begun heading for cover; they will not emerge until the shadows lengthen. Time to halt, pitch camp, break out the beer and sandwiches, tell tall tales of harrowing adventures with maddened buffaloes and edgy elephants. But not quite yet. The marchers come over a low hill and see, in the long sloping hollow beyond, a flock of ostriches and several hundred grazing zebras. As the humans appear, the ostriches begin slowly and warily to move off, but the zebras, altogether unafraid, continue to graze. Ngiri points and says, "*Piga quagga, bwana.*"

"Just a bunch of zebras," Zacharias says.

Gracchus shakes his head. "No. Listen. You hear the sound?"

At first no one perceives anything unusual. But then, yes, Sybille hears it: a shrill barking neigh, very strange, a sound out of lost time, the cry of some beast she has never known. It is a song of the dead. Nerita hears it too, and Mortimer, and finally Zacharias. Gracchus nods toward the far side of the hollow. There, among the zebras, are half a dozen animals that might almost be zebras, but are not—unfinished zebras, striped only on their heads and foreparts; the rest of their bodies are yellowish-brown, their legs are white, their manes are dark brown with pale stripes. Their coats sparkle like mica in the sunshine. Now and again they lift their heads, emit that weird percussive whistling snort, and bend to the grass again. Quaggas. Strays out of the past, relicts, rekindled specters. Gracchus signals and the party fans out along the peak of the hill. Ngiri hands Zacharias his colossal gun. Zacharias kneels, sights.

"No hurry," Gracchus murmurs. "We have all afternoon."

"Do I seem to be hurrying?" Zacharias asks. The zebras now block the little group of quaggas from his view, almost as if by design. He must not shoot a zebra, of course, or there will be trouble with the rangers. Minutes go by. Then the screen of zebras abruptly parts and Zacharias squeezes his trigger. There is a vast explosion; zebras bolt in ten directions, so that the eye is bombarded with dizzying stroboscopic waves of black and white; when the convulsive confusion passes, one of the quaggas is lying on its side, alone in the field, having made the transition across the interface. Sybille regards it calmly. Death once dismayed her, death of any kind, but no longer.

"Piga m'uzuri!" the porters cry exultantly.

"*Kufa*," Gracchus says. "Dead. A neat shot. You have your trophy."

Ngiri is quick with the skinning-knife. That night, camping below Kilimanjaro's broad flank, they dine on roast quagga, deads and porters alike. The meat is juicy, robust, faintly tangy.

Late the following afternoon, as they pass through cooler stream-broken country thick with tall, scrubby gray-green vase-shaped trees, they come upon a monstrosity, a shaggy shambling thing twelve or fifteen feet high, standing upright on ponderous hind legs and balancing itself on an incredibly thick, heavy tail. It leans against a tree, pulling at its top branches with long forelimbs that are tipped with ferocious claws like a row of sickles; it munches voraciously on leaves and twigs. Briefly it notices them, and looks around, studying them with small stupid yellow eyes; then it returns to its meal.

"A rarity," Gracchus says. "I know hunters who have been all over this park without ever running into one. Have you ever seen anything so ugly?"

"What is it?" Sybille asks.

"Megatherium. Giant ground sloth. South American, really, but we weren't fussy about geography when we were stocking this place. We have only four of them, and it costs God knows how many thousands of dollars to shoot one. Nobody's signed up for a ground sloth yet. I doubt anyone will."

Sybille wonders where the beast might be vulnerable to a bullet: surely not in its dim peanut-sized brain. She wonders, too, what sort of sportsman would find pleasure in killing such a thing. For a while they watch as the sluggish monster tears the tree apart. Then they move on.

Gracchus shows them another prodigy at sundown: a pale dome, like some huge melon, nestling in a mound of dense grass beside a stream. "Ostrich egg?" Mortimer guesses.

"Close. Very close. It's a moa egg. World's biggest bird. From New Zealand, extinct since about the eighteenth century."

Nerita crouches and lightly taps the egg. "What an omelet we could make!"

"There's enough there to feed seventy-five of us," Gracchus says. "Two gallons of fluid, easy. But of course we mustn't meddle with it. Natural increase is very important in keeping this park stocked."

"And where's mama moa?" Sybille asks. "Should she have abandoned the egg?"

"Moas aren't very bright," Gracchus answers. "That's one good reason why they became extinct. She must have wandered off to find some dinner. And—"

"Good God," Zacharias blurts.

The moa has returned, emerging suddenly from a thicket. She stands like a feathered mountain above them, limned by the deep blue of twilight: an ostrich, more or less, but a magnified ostrich, an ultimate ostrich, a bird a dozen feet high, with a heavy rounded body and a great thick hose of a neck and taloned legs sturdy as saplings. Surely this is Sinbad's rukh, that can fly off with elephants in its grasp! The bird peers at them, sadly contemplating the band of small beings clustered about her egg; she arches her neck as though readying for attack, and Zacharias reaches for one of the rifles, but Gracchus checks his hand, for the moa is merely rearing back to protest. It utters a deep mournful mooing sound and does not move. "Just back slowly away," Gracchus tells them. "It won't attack. But keep away from the feet; one kick can kill you."

"I was going to apply for a license on a moa," Mortimer says.

"Killing them's a bore," Gracchus tells him. "They just stand there and let you shoot. You're better off with what you signed up for."

What Mortimer has signed up for is an aurochs, the vanished wild ox of the European forests, known to Caesar, known to Pliny, hunted by the hero Siegfried, altogether exterminated by the year 1627. The plains of East Africa are not a comfortable environment for the aurochs and the herd that has been conjured by the genetic necromancers keeps to itself in the wooded highlands, several days' journey from the haunts of quaggas and ground sloths. In this dark grove the hunters come upon troops of chattering baboons and solitary big-eared elephants and, in a place of broken sunlight and shadow, a splendid antelope, a bull bongo with a fine curving pair of horns. Gracchus leads them onward, deeper in. He seems tense: there is peril here. The porters slip through the forest like black wraiths, spreading out in arching crab-claw patterns, communicating with one another and with Gracchus by whistling. Everyone keeps weapons ready in here. Sybille half expects to see leopards draped on overhanging branches, cobras slithering through the undergrowth. But she feels no fear.

They approach a clearing.

"Aurochs," Gracchus says.

A dozen of them are cropping the shrubbery: big short-haired long-horned cattle, muscular and alert. Picking up the scent of the intruders, they lift their heavy heads, sniff, glare. Gracchus and Ngiri confer with eyebrows. Nodding, Gracchus mutters to Mortimer, "Too many of them. Wait for them to thin off." Mortimer smiles. He looks a little nervous. The aurochs has a reputation for attacking without warning. Four, five, six of the beasts slip away, and the others withdraw to the edge of the clearing, as if to plan strategy; but one big bull, sour-eyed and grim, stands his ground, glowering. Gracchus rolls on the balls of his feet. His burly body seems, to Sybille, a study in mobility, in preparedness.

"Now," he says.

In the same moment the bull aurochs charges, moving with extraordinary swiftness, head lowered, horns extended like spears. Mortimer fires. The bullet strikes with a loud whonking sound, crashing into the shoulder of the aurochs, a perfect shot, but the animal does not fall, and Mortimer shoots again, less gracefully ripping into the belly, and then Gracchus and Ngiri are firing also, not at Mortimer's aurochs but over the heads of the others, to drive them away, and the risky tactic works, for the other animals go stampeding off into the woods. The one Mortimer has shot continues toward him, staggering now, losing momentum, and falls practically at his feet, rolling over, knifing the forest floor with its hooves.

"*Kufa,*" Ngiri says. "*Piga nyati m'uzuri, bwana.*" Mortimer grins. "*Piga,*" he says.

Gracchus salutes him. "More exciting than moa," he says.

"And these are mine," says Nerita three hours later, indicating a tree at the outer rim of the forest. Several hundred large pigeons nest in its boughs, so many of them that the tree seems to be sprouting birds rather than leaves. The females are plain—light brown above, gray below—but the males are flamboyant, with rich, glossy blue plumage on their wings and backs, breasts of a wine-red chestnut color, iridescent spots of bronze and green on their necks, and weird, vivid eyes of a bright, fiery orange. Gracchus says, "Right. You've found your passenger pigeons."

"Where's the thrill in shooting pigeons out of a tree?" Mortimer asks.

Nerita gives him a withering look. "Where's the thrill in gunning down a charging bull?" She signals to Ngiri, who fires a shot into the air. The startled pigeons burst from their perches and fly in low circles. In the old days, a century and a half ago in the forests of North America, no one troubled to shoot passenger pigeons on the wing: the pigeons were food, not sport, and it was simpler to blast them as they sat, for that way a single hunter might kill thousands of birds in one day. Thus it took only fifty years to reduce the passenger pigeon population from uncountable sky-blackening billions to zero. Nerita is more sporting. This is a test of her skill, after all. She aims her shotgun, shoots, pumps, shoots, pumps. Stunned birds drop to the ground. She and her gun are a single entity, sharing one purpose. In moments it is all over. The porters retrieve the fallen birds and snap their necks. Nerita has the dozen pigeons her license allows: a pair to mount, the rest for tonight's dinner. The survivors have returned to their tree and stare placidly, unreproachfully, at the hunters. "They breed so damned fast," Gracchus mutters. "If we aren't careful, they'll be getting out of the preserve and taking over all of Africa."

Sybille laughs. "Don't worry. We'll cope. We wiped them out once and we can do it again, if we have to."

Sybille's prey is a dodo. In Dar, when they were applying for their licenses, the others mocked her choice: a fat flightless bird, unable to run or fight, so feeble of wit that it fears nothing. She ignored them. She wants a dodo because to her it is the essence of extinction, the prototype of all that is dead and vanished. That there is no sport in shooting foolish dodos means little to Sybille. Hunting itself is meaningless for her.

Through this vast park she wanders as in a dream. She sees ground sloths, great auks, quaggas, moas, heath hens, Javan rhinos, giant armadillos, and many other rarities. The place is an abode of ghosts. The ingenuities of the genetic craftsmen are limitless; someday, perhaps, the preserve will offer trilobites, tyrannosaurs, mastodons, saber-toothed cats, baluchitheria, even—why not?—packs of australopithecines, tribes of Neanderthals. For the amusement of the deads, whose games tend to be somber. Sybille wonders whether it can really be considered killing, this slaughter of laboratory-spawned novelties. Are these animals real or artificial? Living things, or cleverly animated constructs? Real, she decides. Living. They eat, they metabolize, they reproduce. They must seem real to themselves, and so they are real, realer, maybe, than dead human beings who walk again in their own cast-off bodies.

"Shotgun," Sybille says to the closest porter.

There is the bird, ugly, ridiculous, waddling laboriously through the tall grass. Sybille accepts a weapon and sights along its barrel. "Wait," Nerita says. "I'd like to get a picture of this." She moves slantwise around the group, taking exaggerated care not to frighten the dodo, but the dodo does not seem to be aware of any of them. Like an emissary from the realm of darkness, carrying good news of death to those creatures not yet extinct, it plods diligently across their path. "Fine," Nerita says. "Anthony, point at the dodo will you, as if you've just noticed it? Kent, I'd like you to look down at your gun, study its bolt or something. Fine. And Sybille, just hold that pose—aiming—yes—"

Nerita takes the picture.

Calmly Sybille pulls the trigger.

"*Kazi imekwisha*," Gracchus says. "The work is finished."

6.

Although to be driven back upon oneself is an uneasy affair at best, rather like trying to cross a border with borrowed credentials, it seems to be now the one condition necessary to the beginnings of real self-respect. Most of our platitudes notwithstanding, self-deception remains the most difficult deception. The tricks that work on others count for nothing in that very well-lit back alley where one keeps assignations with oneself: no winning smiles will do here, no prettily drawn lists of good intentions.

Joan Didion: On Self-Respect

"You better believe what Jeej is trying to tell you," Dolorosa said. "Ten minutes inside the Cold Town, they'll have your number. Five minutes."

Jijibhoi's man was small, rumpled-looking, forty or fifty years old, with untidy long dark hair and wide-set smoldering eyes. His skin was sallow and his face was gaunt. Such other deads as Klein had seen at close range had about them an air of unearthly serenity, but not this one: Dolorosa was tense, fidgety, a knuckle-cracker, a lip-gnawer. Yet somehow there could be no doubt he was a dead, as much a dead as Zacharias, as Gracchus, as Mortimer.

"They'll have my what?" Klein asked.

"Your number. Your number. They'll know you aren't a dead, because it can't be faked. Jesus, don't you even speak English? Jorge, that's a foreign name. I should have known. Where are you from?"

"Argentina, as a matter of fact, but I was brought to California when I was a small boy. In 1955. Look, if they catch me, they catch me. I just want to get in there and spend half an hour talking with my wife."

"Mister, you don't have any wife any more."

"With Sybille," Klein said, exasperated. "To talk with Sybille, my—my former wife."

"All right. I'll get you inside."

"What will it cost?"

"Never mind that," Dolorosa said. "I owe Jeej here a few favors. More than a few. So I'll get you the drug—"

"Drug?"

"The drug the Treasury agents use when they infiltrate the Cold Towns. It narrows the pupils, contracts the capillaries, gives you that good old zombie look. The agents always get caught and thrown out, and so will you, but at least you'll go in there feeling that you've got a convincing disguise. Little oily capsule, one every morning before breakfast."

Klein looked at Jijibhoi. "Why do Treasury agents infiltrate the Cold Towns?"

"For the same reasons they infiltrate anywhere else," Jijibhoi said. "To spy. They are trying to compile dossiers on the financial dealings of the deads, you see, and until proper life-defining legislation is approved by Congress there is no precise way of compelling a person who is deemed legally dead to divulge—"

Dolorosa said, "Next, the background. I can get you a card of residence from Albany Cold Town in New York. You died last December, okay, and they rekindled you back east because—let's see—"

"I could have been attending the annual meeting of the American Historical Association in New York," Klein suggested. "That's what I do, you understand, professor of contemporary history at UCLA. Because of the Christmas holiday my body couldn't be shipped back to California, no room on any flight, and so they took me to Albany. How does that sound?"

Dolorosa smiled. "You really enjoy making up lies, professor, don't you? I can dig that quality in you. Okay, Albany Cold Town, and this is your first trip out of there, your drying-off trip—that's what it's called, drying-off—you come out of the Cold Town like a new butterfly just out of its cocoon, all soft and damp, and you're on your own in a strange place. Now, there's a lot of stuff you'll need to know about how to behave, little mannerisms, social graces, that kind of crap, and I'll work on that with you tomorrow and Wednesday and Friday, three sessions; that ought to be enough. Meanwhile let me give you the basics. There are only three things you really have to remember while you're inside:

"1) Never ask a direct question.

"2) Never lean on anybody's arm. You know what I mean?

"3) Keep in mind that to a dead the whole universe is plastic, nothing's real, nothing matters a hell of a lot, it's all only a joke. Only a joke, friend, only a joke."

Early in April he flew to Salt Lake City, rented a car, and drove out past Moab into the high plateau rimmed by red-rock mountains where the deads had built Zion Cold Town. This was Klein's second visit to the necropolis. The other had been in the late summer of '91, a hot, parched season when the sun filled half the sky and even the gnarled junipers looked dazed from thirst; but now it was a frosty afternoon, with faint pale light streaming out of the wintry western hills and occasional gusts of light snow whirling through the iron-blue air. Jijibhoi's route instructions pulsed from the memo screen on his dashboard. Fourteen miles from town, yes, narrow paved lane turns off highway, yes, discreet little sign announcing PRIVATE ROAD, NO ADMITTANCE, yes, a second sign a thousand yards in, ZION COLD TOWN, MEMBERS ONLY, yes, and then just beyond that the barrier of green light across the road, the scanner system, the roadblocks sliding like scythes out of the underground installations, a voice on an invisible loudspeaker saying, "If you have a permit to enter Zion Cold Town, please place it under your left-hand windshield wiper."

That other time he had had no permit, and he had gone no farther than this, though at least he had managed a little colloquy with the unseen gatekeeper out of which he had squeezed the information that Sybille was indeed living in that particular Cold Town. This time he affixed Dolorosa's forged card of residence to his windshield, and waited tensely, and in thirty seconds the roadblocks slid from sight. He drove on, along a winding road that followed the natural contours of a dense forest of scrubby conifers, and came at last to a brick wall that curved away into the trees as though it encircled the entire town. Probably it did. Klein had an overpowering sense of the Cold Town as a hermetic city, ponderous and sealed as old Egypt. There was a metal gate in the brick wall; green electronic eyes surveyed him, signaled their approval, and the wall rolled open.

He drove slowly toward the center of town, passing through a zone of what he supposed were utility buildings—storage depots, a power substation, the municipal waterworks, whatever, a bunch of grim windowless one-story cinderblock affairs—and then into the residential district, which was not much lovelier. The streets were laid out on a rectangular grid; the buildings were squat, dreary, impersonal, homogeneous. There was practically no automobile traffic, and in a dozen blocks he saw no more than ten pedestrians, who did not even glance at him. So this was the environment in which the deads chose to spend their second lives. But why such deliberate bleakness? "You will never understand us," Dolorosa had warned. Dolorosa was right. Jijibhoi had told him that Cold Towns were something less than charming, but Klein had not been prepared for this. There was a glacial quality about the place, as though it were wholly entombed in a block of clear ice: silence, sterility, a mortuary calm. Cold Town, yes, aptly named. Architecturally, the town looked like the worst of all possible cheap-and-sleazy tract developments, but the psychic texture it projected was even more depressing, more like that of one of those ghastly retirement communities, one of the innumerable Leisure Worlds or Sun Manors, those childless joyless retreats where colonies of that other kind of living dead collected to await the last trumpet. Klein shivered.

At last, another few minutes deeper into the town, a sign of activity, if not exactly of life: a shopping center, flat-topped brown stucco buildings around a U-shaped courtyard, a steady flow of shoppers moving about. All right. His first test was about to commence. He parked his car near the mouth of the

U and strolled uneasily inward. He felt as if his forehead were a beacon, flashing glowing betrayals at rhythmic intervals:

FRAUD INTRUDER INTERLOPER SPY

Go ahead, he thought, seize me, seize the impostor, get it over with, throw me out, string me up, crucify me. But no one seemed to pick up the signals. He was altogether ignored. Out of courtesy? Or just contempt? He stole what he hoped were covert glances at the shoppers, half expecting to run across Sybille right away. They all looked like sleepwalkers, moving in glazed silence about their errands. No smiles, no chatter: the icy aloofness of these self-contained people heightened the familiar suburban atmosphere of the shopping center into surrealist intensity, Norman Rockwell with an overlay of Dali or De Chirico. The shopping center looked like all other shopping centers: clothing stores, a bank, a record shop, snack bars, a florist, a TV-stereo outlet, a theater, a five-and-dime. One difference, though, became apparent as Klein wandered from shop to shop: the whole place was automated. There were no clerks anywhere, only the ubiquitous data screens, and no doubt a battery of hidden scanners to discourage shoplifters. (Or did the impulse toward petty theft perish with the body's first death?) The customers selected all the merchandise themselves, checked it out via data screens, touched their thumbs to charge-plates to debit their accounts. Of course. No one was going to waste his precious rekindled existence standing behind a counter to sell tennis shoes or cotton candy. Nor were the dwellers in the Cold Towns likely to dilute their isolation by hiring a labor force of imported warms. Somebody here had to do a little work, obviously—how did the merchandise get into the stores?—but, in general,

Klein realized, what could not be done here by machines would not be done at all.

For ten minutes he prowled the center. Just when he was beginning to think he must be entirely invisible to these people, a short, broad-shouldered man, bald but with oddly youthful features, paused in front of him and said, "I am Pablo. I welcome you to Zion Cold Town." This unexpected puncturing of the silence so startled Klein that he had to fight to retain appropriate deadlike imperturbability. Pablo smiled warmly and touched both his hands to Klein's in friendly greeting, but his eyes were frigid, hostile, remote, a terrifying contradiction. "I've been sent to bring you to the lodging-place. Come: your car."

Other than to give directions, Pablo spoke only three times during the five-minute drive. "Here is the rekindling house," he said. A five-story building, as inviting as a hospital, with walls of dark bronze and windows black as onyx. "This is Guidefather's house," Pablo said a moment later. A modest brick building, like a rectory, at the edge of a small park. And, finally: "This is where you will stay. Enjoy your visit." Abruptly he got out of the car and walked rapidly away.

This was the house of strangers, the hotel for visiting deads, a long low cinderblock structure, functional and unglamorous, one of the least seductive buildings in this city of stark disagreeable buildings. However else it might be with the deads, they clearly had no craving for fancy architecture. A voice out of a data screen in the spartan lobby assigned him to a room: a white-walled box, square, high of ceiling. He had his own toilet, his own data screen, a narrow bed, a chest of drawers, a modest closet, a small window that gave him a view of a neighboring building just as drab as this. Nothing had been said about rental; perhaps he was a guest of the city. Nothing had been said about anything. It seemed that he had been accepted. So much for Jijibhoi's gloomy assurance that he would instantly be found out, so much for Dolorosa's insistence that they would have his number in ten minutes or less. He had been in Zion Cold Town for half an hour. Did they have his number?

"Eating isn't important among us," Dolorosa had said.

"But you do eat?"

"Of course we eat. It just isn't *important*."

It was important to Klein, though. Not haute cuisine, necessarily, but some sort of food, preferably three times a day. He was getting hungry now. Ring for room service? There were no servants in this city. He turned to the data screen. Dolorosa's first rule: *Never ask a direct question.* Surely that didn't apply to the data screen, only to his fellow deads. He didn't have to observe the niceties of etiquette when talking to a computer. Still, the voice behind the screen might not be that of a computer after all, so he tried to employ the oblique, elliptical conversational style that Dolorosa said the deads favored among themselves:

"Dinner?"

"Commissary."

"Where?"

"Central Four," said the screen.

Central Four? All right. He would find the way. He changed into fresh clothing and went down the long vinyl-floored hallway to the lobby. Night had come; streetlamps were glowing; under cloak of darkness the city's ugliness was no longer so obtrusive, and there was even a kind of controlled beauty about the brutal regularity of its streets.

The streets were unmarked, though, and deserted. Klein walked at random for ten minutes, hoping to meet someone heading for the Central Four commissary. But when he did come upon someone, a tall and regal woman well advanced in years, he found himself incapable of approaching her. (*Never ask a direct question. Never lean on anybody's arm.*) He walked alongside her, in silence and at a distance, until she turned suddenly to enter a house. For ten minutes more he wandered alone again. This is ridiculous, he thought: dead or warm, I'm a stranger in town, I should be entitled to a little assistance. Maybe Dolorosa was just trying to complicate things. On the next corner, when Klein caught sight of a man hunched away from the wind, lighting a cigarette, he went boldly over to him.

"Excuse me, but—"

The other looked up. "Klein?" he said. "Yes. Of course. Well, so you've made the crossing too!"

He was one of Sybille's Zanzibar companions, Klein realized. The quick-eyed, sharp-edged one—Mortimer. A member of her pseudo-familial grouping, whatever that might be. Klein stared sullenly at him. This had to be the moment when his imposture would be exposed, for only some six weeks had passed since he had argued with Mortimer in the gardens of Sybille's Zanzibar hotel, not nearly enough time for someone to have died and been rekindled and gone through his drying-off. But a moment passed and Mortimer said nothing. At length Klein said, "I just got here. Pablo showed me to the house of strangers and now I'm looking for the commissary."

"Central Four? I'm going there myself. How lucky for you." No sign of suspicion in Mortimer's face. Perhaps an elusive smile revealed his awareness that Klein could not be what he claimed to be. *Keep in mind that to a dead the whole universe is plastic, it's all only a joke.* "I'm waiting for Nerita," Mortimer said. "We can all eat together."

Klein said heavily, "I was rekindled in Albany Cold Town. I've just emerged."

"How nice," Mortimer said.

Nerita Tracy stepped out of a building just beyond the corner—a slim athletic-looking woman, about forty, with short reddish-brown hair. As she swept toward them Mortimer said, "Here's Klein, who we met in Zanzibar. Just rekindled, out of Albany."

"Sybille will be amused."

"Is she in town?" Klein blurted.

Mortimer and Nerita exchanged sly glances. Klein felt abashed. *Never ask a direct question.* Damn Dolorosa!

Nerita said, "You'll see her before long. Shall we go to dinner?"

The commissary was less austere than Klein had expected: actually quite an inviting restaurant, elaborately constructed on five or six levels divided by lustrous dark hangings into small, secluded dining areas. It had the warm, rich look of a tropical resort. But the food, which came automat-style out of revolving dispensers, was prefabricated and cheerless—another jarring contradiction. *Only a joke, friend, only a joke.* In any case he was less hungry than he had imagined at the hotel. He sat with Mortimer and Nerita, picking at his meal, while their conversation flowed past him at several times the speed of thought. They spoke in fragments and ellipses, in periphrastics and aposiopeses, in a style abundant in chiasmus, metonymy, meiosis, oxymoron, and zeugma; their dazzling rhetorical techniques left him baffled and uncomfortable, which beyond much doubt was their intention. Now and again they would dart from a thicket of indirection to skewer him with a quick corroborative stab: Isn't that so, they would say, and he would smile and nod, nod and smile, saying, Yes, yes, absolutely. Did they know he was a fake, and were they merely playing with him, or had they, somehow, impossibly, accepted him as one of them? So subtle was their style that he could not tell. A very new member of the society of the rekindled, he told himself, would be nearly as much at sea here as a warm in deadface.

Then Nerita said—no verbal games, this time—"You still miss her terribly, don't you?"

"I do. Some things evidently never perish."

"Everything perishes," Mortimer said. "The dodo, the aurochs, the Holy Roman Empire, the T'ang Dynasty, the walls of Byzantium, the language of Mohenjodaro."

"But not the Great Pyramid, the Yangtze, the coelacanth, or the skullcap of Pithecanthropus," Klein countered. "Some things persist and endure. And some can be regenerated. Lost languages have been deciphered. I believe the dodo and the aurochs are hunted in a certain African park in this very era."

"Replicas," Mortimer said.

"Convincing replicas. Simulations as good as the original."

"Is that what you want?" Nerita asked.

"I want what's possible to have."

"A convincing replica of lost love?"

"I might be willing to settle for five minutes of conversation with her."

"You'll have it. Not tonight. See? There she is. But don't bother her now." Nerita nodded across the gulf in the center of the restaurant; on the far side, three levels up from where they sat, Sybille and Kent Zacharias had appeared. They stood for a brief while at the edge of their dining alcove, staring blandly and emotionlessly into the restaurant's central well. Klein felt a muscle jerking uncontrollably in his cheek, a damning revelation of undeadlike uncoolness, and pressed his hand over it, so that it twanged and throbbed against his palm. She was like a goddess up there, manifesting herself in her sanctum to her worshippers, a pale shimmering figure, more beautiful even than she had become to him through the anguished enhancements of memory, and it seemed impossible to him that that being had ever been his wife, that he had known her when her eyes were puffy and reddened from a night of study, that he had looked down at her face as they made love and had seen her lips pull back in that spasm of ecstasy that is so close to a grimace of pain, that he had known her crochety and unkind in her illness, short-tempered and impatient in health, a person of flaws and weaknesses, of odors and blemishes, in short a human being, this goddess, this unreal rekindled creature, this object of his quest, this Sybille. Serenely she turned, serenely she vanished into her cloaked alcove. "She knows you're here," Nerita told him. "You'll see her. Perhaps tomorrow." Then Mortimer said something maddeningly oblique, and Nerita replied with the same off-center mystification, and Klein once more was plunged into the river of their easy dancing wordplay, down into it, down and down and down, and as he struggled to keep from drowning, as he fought to comprehend their interchanges, he never once looked toward the place where Sybille sat, not even once, and congratulated himself on having accomplished that much at least in his masquerade.

That night, lying alone in his room at the house of strangers, he wonders what he will say to Sybille when they finally meet, and what she will say to him. Will he dare bluntly to ask her to describe to him the quality of her new existence? That is all that he wants from her, really, that knowledge, that opening of an aperture into her transfigured self; that is as much as he hopes to get from her, knowing as he does that there is scarcely a chance of regaining her, but will he dare to ask, will he dare even that? Of course his asking such things will reveal to her that he is still a warm, too dense and gross of perception to comprehend the life of a dead; but he is certain she will sense that anyway, instantly. What will he say, what will he say? He plays out an imagined script of their conversation in the theater of his mind:

—Tell me what it's like, Sybille, to be the way you are now.

—Like swimming under a sheet of glass.

—I don't follow.

—Everything is quiet where I am, Jorge. There's a peace that passeth all understanding. I used to feel sometimes that I was caught up in a great storm, that I was being buffeted by every breeze, that my life was being consumed by agitations and frenzies, but now, now, I'm at the eye of the storm, at the place where everything is always calm. I observe rather than let myself be acted upon.

—But isn't there a loss of feeling that way? Don't you feel that you're wrapped in an insulating layer? Like swimming under glass, you say—that conveys being insulated, being cut off, being almost numb.

—I suppose you might think so. The way it is is that one no longer is affected by the unnecessary.

—It sounds to me like a limited existence.

—Less limited than the grave, Jorge.

—I never understood why you wanted rekindling. You were such a world-devourer, Sybille, you lived with such intensity, such passion. To settle for the kind of existence you have now, to be only half alive—

—Don't be a fool, Jorge. To be half alive is better than to be rotting in the ground. I was so young. There was so much else still to see and do.

—But to see it and do it half alive?

—Those were your words, not mine. I'm not alive at all. I'm neither less nor more than the person you knew. I'm another kind of being altogether. Neither less nor more, only different.

—Are all your perceptions different?

—Very much so. My perspective is broader. Little things stand revealed as little things.

—Give me an example, Sybille.

—I'd rather not. How could I make anything clear to you? Die and be with us, and you'll understand.

—You know I'm not dead?

—Oh, Jorge, how funny you are!

—How nice that I can still amuse you.

—You look so hurt, so tragic. I could almost feel sorry for you. Come: ask me anything.

—Could you leave your companions and live in the world again?

—I've never considered that.

—Could you?

—I suppose I could. But why should I? This is my world now.

—This ghetto.

—Is that how it seems to you?

—You lock yourselves into a closed society of your peers, a tight subculture. Your own jargon, your own wall of etiquette and idiosyncrasy. Designed, I think, mainly to keep the outsiders off balance, to keep them feeling like outsiders. It's a defensive thing. The hippies, the blacks, the gays, the deads—same mechanism, same process.

—The Jews, too. Don't forget the Jews.

—All right, Sybille, the Jews. With their little tribal jokes, their special holidays, their own mysterious language, yes, a good case in point.

—So I've joined a new tribe. What's wrong with that?

—Did you need to be part of a tribe?

—What did I have before? The tribe of Californians? The tribe of academics?

—The tribe of Jorge and Sybille Klein.

—Too narrow. Anyway, I've been expelled from that tribe. I needed to join another one.

—Expelled?

—By death. After that there's no going back.

—You could go back. Any time.

—Oh, no, no, no, Jorge, I can't, I can't, I'm not Sybille Klein any more. I never will be again. How can I explain it to you? There's no way. Death brings on changes. Die and see, Jorge. Die and see.

Nerita said, "She's waiting for you in the lounge."

It was a big, coldly furnished room at the far end of the other wing of the house of strangers. Sybille stood by a window through which pale, chilly morning light was streaming. Mortimer was with her, and also Kent Zacharias. The two men favored Klein with mysterious oblique smiles—courteous or derisive, he could not tell which. "Do you like our town?" Zacharias asked. "Have you been seeing the sights?" Klein chose not to reply. He acknowledged the question with a faint nod and turned to Sybille. Strangely, he felt altogether calm at this moment of attaining a years-old desire: he felt nothing at all in her presence, no panic, no yearning, no dismay, no nostalgia, nothing, nothing. As though he were truly a dead. He knew it was the tranquillity of utter terror.

"We'll leave you two alone," Zacharias said. "You must have so much to tell each other." He went out, with Nerita and Mortimer. Klein's eyes met Sybille's and lingered there. She was looking at him coolly, in a kind of impersonal appraisal. That damnable smile of hers, Klein thought: dying turns them all into Mona Lisas.

She said, "Do you plan to stay here long?"

"Probably not. A few days, maybe a week." He moistened his lips. "How have you been, Sybille? How has it been going?"

"It's all been about as I expected."

What do you mean by that? Can you give me some details? Are you at all disappointed? Have there been any surprises? What has it been like for you, Sybille? Oh, Jesus—

—Never ask a direct question—

He said, "I wish you had let me visit with you in Zanzibar."

"That wasn't possible. Let's not talk about it now." She dismissed the episode with a casual wave. After a moment she said, "Would you like to hear a fascinating story I've uncovered about the early days of Omani influence in Zanzibar?"

The impersonality of the question startled him. How could she display such absolute lack of curiosity about his presence in Zion Cold Town, his claim to be a dead, his reasons for wanting to see her? How could she plunge so quickly, so coldly, into a discussion of archaic political events in Zanzibar?

"I suppose so," he said weakly.

"It's a sort of Arabian Nights story, really. It's the story of how Ahmad the Sly overthrew Abdullah ibn Muhammad Alawi."

The names were strange to him. He had indeed taken some small part in her historical researches, but it was years since he had worked with her, and everything had drifted about in his mind, leaving a jumbled residue of Ahmads and Hasans and Abdullahs. "I'm sorry," he said. "I don't recall who they were."

Unperturbed, Sybille said, "Certainly you remember that in the eighteenth and early nineteenth centuries the chief power in the Indian Ocean was the Arab state of Oman, ruled from Muscat on the Persian Gulf. Under the Busaidi dynasty, founded in 1744 by Ahmad ibn Said al-Busaidi, the Omani extended their power to East Africa. The logical capital for their African empire was the port of

Mombasa, but they were unable to evict a rival dynasty reigning there, so the Busaidi looked toward nearby Zanzibar—a cosmopolitan island of mixed Arab, Indian, and African population. Zanzibar's strategic placement on the coast and its spacious and well-protected harbor made it an ideal base for the East African slave trade that the Busaidi of Oman intended to dominate."

"It comes back to me now, I think."

"Very well. The founder of the Omani Sultanate of Zanzibar was Ahmad ibn Majid the Sly, who came to the throne of Oman in 1811—do you remember?—upon the death of his uncle Abd-er-Rahman al-Busaidi."

"The names sound familiar," Klein said doubtfully.

"Seven years later," Sybille continued, "seeking to conquer Zanzibar without the use of force, Ahmad the Sly shaved his beard and mustache and visited the island disguised as a soothsayer, wearing yellow robes and a costly emerald in his turban. At that time most of Zanzibar was governed by a native ruler of mixed Arab and African blood, Abdullah ibn Muhammad Alawi, whose hereditary title was Mwenyi Mkuu. The Mwenyi Mkuu's subjects were mainly Africans, members of a tribe called the Hadimu. Sultan Ahmad, arriving in Zanzibar Town, gave a demonstration of his soothsaying skills on the waterfront and attracted so much attention that he speedily gained an audience at the court of the Mwenyi Mkuu. Ahmad predicted a glowing future for Abdullah, declaring that a powerful prince famed throughout the world would come to Zanzibar, make the Mwenyi Mkuu his high lieutenant, and would confirm him and his descendants as lords of Zanzibar forever.

"'How do you know these things?' asked the Mwenyi Mkuu.

"'There is a potion I drink,' Sultan Ahmad replied, 'that enables me to see what is to come. Do you wish to taste of it?'

"'Most surely I do,' Abdullah said, and Ahmad thereupon gave him a drug that sent him into rapturous transports and showed him visions of paradise. Looking down from his place near the footstool of Allah, the Mwenyi Mkuu saw a rich and happy Zanzibar governed by his children's children's children. For hours he wandered in fantasies of almighty power.

"Ahmad then departed, and let his beard and mustache grow again, and returned to Zanzibar ten weeks later in his full regalia as Sultan of Oman, at the head of an imposing and powerful armada. He went at once to the court of the Mwenyi Mkuu and proposed, just as the soothsayer had prophesied, that Oman and Zanzibar enter into a treaty of alliance under which Oman would assume responsibility for much of Zanzibar's external relations—including the slave trade—while guaranteeing the authority of the Mwenyi Mkuu over domestic affairs. In return for his partial abdication of authority, the Mwenyi Mkuu would receive financial compensation from Oman. Remembering the vision the soothsayer had revealed to him, Abdullah at once signed the treaty, thereby legitimizing what was, in effect, the Omani conquest of Zanzibar. A great feast was held to celebrate the treaty, and, as a mark of honor, the Mwenyi Mkuu offered Sultan Ahmad a rare drug used locally, known as *borgash*, or 'the flower of truth.' Ahmad only pretended to put the pipe to his lips, for he loathed all mind-altering drugs, but Abdullah, as the flower of truth possessed him, looked at Ahmad and recognized the outlines of the soothsayer's face behind the Sultan's new beard. Realizing that he had been deceived, the Mwenyi Mkuu thrust his dagger, the tip of which was poisoned, deep into the Sultan's side and fled the banquet hall, taking up residence on the neighboring island of Pemba. Ahmad ibn Majid survived, but the poison consumed his vital organs and the remaining ten years of his life were spent in constant agony. As for the Mwenyi Mkuu, the Sultan's men hunted him down and put him to death along with ninety members of his family, and native rule in Zanzibar was therewith extinguished."

Sybille paused. "Is that not a gaudy and wonderful story?" she asked at last.

"Fascinating," Klein said. "Where did you find it?"

"Unpublished memoirs of Claude Richburn of the East India Company. Buried deep in the London archives. Strange that no historian ever came upon it before, isn't it? The standard texts simply say that Ahmad used his navy to bully Abdullah into signing the treaty, and then had the Mwenyi Mkuu assassinated at the first convenient moment."

"Very strange," Klein agreed. But he had not come here to listen to romantic tales of visionary potions and royal treacheries. He groped for some way to bring the conversation to a more personal level. Fragments of his imaginary dialogue with Sybille floated through his mind. *Everything is quiet where I am, Jorge. There's a peace that passeth all understanding. Like swimming under a sheet of glass. The way it is is that one no longer is affected by the unnecessary. Little things stand revealed as little things. Die and be with us, and you'll understand.* Yes. Perhaps. But did she really believe any of that? He had put all the words in her mouth; everything he had imagined her to say was his own construct, worthless as a key to the true Sybille. Where would he find the key, though?

She gave him no chance. "I will be going back to Zanzibar soon," she said. "There's much I want to learn about this incident from the people in the back country—old legends about the last days of the Mwenyi Mkuu, perhaps variants on the basic story—"

"May I accompany you?"

"Don't you have your own research to resume, Jorge?" she asked, and did not wait for an answer. She walked briskly toward the door of the lounge and went out, and he was alone.

7.

I mean what they and their hired psychiatrists call "delusional systems." Needless to say, "delusions" are always officially defined. We don't have to worry about questions of real or unreal. They only talk out of expediency. It's the system *that matters. How the data arrange themselves inside it. Some are consistent, others fall apart.*

Thomas Pynchon: Gravity's Rainbow

Once more the deads, this time only three of them coming over on the morning flight from Dar. Three was better than five, Daud Mahmoud Barwani supposed, but three was still more than a sufficiency. Not that those others, two months back, had caused any trouble, staying just the one day and flitting off to the mainland again, but it made him uncomfortable to think of such creatures on the same small island as himself. With all the world to choose, why did they keep coming to Zanzibar?

"The plane is here," said the flight controller.

Thirteen passengers. The health officer let the

local people through the gate first—two newspapermen and four legislators coming back from the Pan-African Conference in Capetown—and then processed a party of four Japanese tourists, unsmiling owlish men festooned with cameras. And then the deads: and Barwani was surprised to discover that they were the same ones as before, the red-haired man, the brown-haired man without the beard, the black-haired woman. Did deads have so much money that they could fly from America to Zanzibar every few months? Barwani had heard a tale to the effect that each new dead, when he rose from his coffin, was presented with bars of gold equal to his own weight, and now he thought he believed it. No good will come of having such beings loose in the world, he told himself, and certainly none from letting them into Zanzibar. Yet he had no choice. "Welcome once again to the isle of cloves," he said unctuously, and smiled a bureaucratic smile, and wondered, not for the first time, what would become of Daud Mahmoud Barwani once his days on earth had reached their end.

"—Ahmad the Sly versus Abdullah Something," Klein said. "That's all she would talk about. The history of Zanzibar." He was in Jijibhoi's study. The night was warm and a late-season rain was falling, blurring the million sparkling lights of the Los Angeles basin. "It would have been, you know, gauche to ask her any direct questions. Gauche. I haven't felt so gauche since I was fourteen. I was helpless among them, a foreigner, a child."

"Do you think they saw through your disguise?" Jijibhoi asked.

"I can't tell. They seemed to be toying with me, to be having sport with me, but that may just have been their general style with any newcomer. Nobody challenged me. Nobody hinted I might be an impostor. Nobody seemed to care very much about me or what I was doing there or how I had happened to become a dead. Sybille and I stood face to face, and I wanted to reach out to her, I wanted her to reach out to me, and there was no contact, none, none at all, it was as though we had just met at some academic cocktail party and the only thing on her mind was the new nugget of obscure history she had just unearthed, and so she told me all about how Sultan Ahmad outfoxed Abdullah and Abdullah stabbed the Sultan." Klein caught sight of a set of familiar books on Jijibhoi's crowded shelves—Oliver and Mathew, *History of East Africa*, books that had traveled everywhere with Sybille in the years of their marriage. He pulled forth Volume I, saying, "She claimed that the standard histories give a sketchy and inaccurate description of the incident and that she's only now discovered the true story. For all I know, she was just playing a game with me, telling me a piece of established history as though it were something nobody knew till last week. Let me see—Ahmad, Ahmad, Ahmad—"

He examined the index. Five Ahmads were listed, but there was no entry for a Sultan Ahmad ibn Majid the Sly. Indeed an Ahmad ibn Majid was cited, but he was mentioned only in a footnote and appeared to be an Arab chronicler. Klein found three Abdullahs, none of them a man of Zanzibar. "Something's wrong," he murmured.

"It does not matter, dear Jorge," Jijibhoi said mildly.

"It does. Wait a minute." He prowled the listings. Under *Zanzibar, Rulers,* he found no Ahmads, no Abdullahs; he did discover a Majid ibn Said, but when he checked the reference he found that he had reigned somewhere in the second half of the nineteenth century. Desperately Klein flipped pages, skimming, turning back, searching. Eventually he looked up and said, "It's all wrong!"

"The Oxford History of East Africa?"

"The details of Sybille's story. Look, she said this Ahmad the Sly gained the throne of Oman in 1811, and seized Zanzibar seven years later. But the book says that a certain Seyyid Said al-Busaidi became Sultan of Oman in 1806, and ruled for *fifty years.* He was the one, not this nonexistent Ahmad the Sly, who grabbed Zanzibar, but he did it in 1828, and the ruler he compelled to sign a treaty with him, the Mwenyi Mkuu, was named Hasan ibn Ahmad Alawi, and—" Klein shook his head. "It's an altogether different cast of characters. No stabbings, no assassinations, the dates are entirely different, the whole thing—"

Jijibhoi smiled sadly. "The deads are often mischievous."

"But why would she invent a complete fantasy and palm it off as a sensational new discovery? Sybille was the most scrupulous scholar I ever knew! She would never—"

"That was the Sybille you knew, dear friend. I keep urging you to realize that this is another person, a new person, within her body."

"A person who would lie about history?"

"A person who would tease," Jijibhoi said.

"Yes," Klein muttered. "Who would tease." *Keep in mind that to a dead the whole universe is plastic, nothing's real, nothing matters a hell of a lot.* "Who would tease a stupid, boring, annoyingly persistent ex-husband who has shown up in her Cold Town, wearing a transparent disguise and pretending to be a dead. Who would invent not only an anecdote but even its principals, as a joke, a game, a *jeu d'esprit.* Oh, God. Oh, God, how cruel she is, how foolish I was! It was her way of telling me she knew I was a phony dead. *Quid pro quo,* fraud for fraud!"

"What will you do?"

"I don't know," Klein said.

What he did, against Jijibhoi's strong advice and his own better judgment, was to get more pills from Dolorosa and return to Zion Cold Town. There would be a fitful joy, like that of probing the socket of a missing tooth, in confronting Sybille with the evidence of her fictional Ahmad, her imaginary Abdullah. Let there be no more games between us, he would say. Tell me what I need to know, Sybille, and then let me go away; but tell me only truth. All the way to Utah he rehearsed his speech, polishing and embellishing. There was no need for it, though, since this time the gate of Zion Cold Town would not open for him. The scanners scanned his forged Albany card and the loudspeaker said, "Your credentials are invalid."

Which could have ended it. He might have returned to Los Angeles and picked up the pieces of his life. All this semester he had been on sabbatical leave, but the summer term was coming and there was work to do. He did return to Los Angeles, but only long enough to pack a somewhat larger suitcase, find his passport, and drive to the airport. On a sweet May evening a BOAC jet took him over the Pole to London, where, barely pausing for coffee and buns at an airport shop, he boarded another plane that carried him southeast toward Africa. More asleep than awake he watched the dreamy landmarks drifting past: the Mediterranean, coming and going with surprising rapidity, and the tawny carpet of the Libyan Desert, and the mighty Nile, reduced to a brown thread's thickness when viewed from a height of ten miles. Suddenly Kilimanjaro, mist-wrapped, snowbound, loomed like a giant double-headed blister to his right, far below, and he thought he could make out to his left the distant glare of the sun on the Indian Ocean. Then the big needle-nosed plane began its abrupt swooping descent, and he found himself, soon after, stepping out into the warm humid air and dazzling sunlight of Dar es Salaam.

Too soon, too soon. He felt unready to go on to Zanzibar. A day or two of rest, perhaps: he picked a Dar hotel at random, the Agip, liking the strange sound of its name, and hired a taxi. The hotel was sleek and clean, a streamlined affair in the glossy 1960's style, much cheaper than the Kilimanjaro where he had stayed briefly on the other trip, and located in a pleasant leafy quarter of the city, near the ocean. He strolled about for a short while, discovered that he was altogether exhausted, returned to his room for a nap that stretched on for nearly five hours, and, awaking groggy, showered and dressed for dinner. The hotel's dining room was full of beefy red-faced fair-haired men, jacketless and wearing open-throated white shirts, all of whom reminded him disturbingly of Kent Zacharias; but these were warms, Britishers from their accents, engineers, he suspected, from their conversation. They were building a dam and a power plant somewhere up the coast, it seemed, or perhaps a power plant without a dam; it was hard to follow what they said. They drank a good deal of gin and spoke in hearty booming shouts. There were also a good many Japanese businessmen, of course, looking trim and restrained in dark blue suits and narrow ties, and at the table next to Klein's were five tanned curly-haired men talking in rapid Hebrew—Israelis, surely. The only Africans in sight were waiters and bartenders. Klein ordered Mombasa oysters, steak, and a carafe of red wine, and found the food unexpectedly good, but left most of it on his plate. It was late evening in Tanzania, but for him it was ten o'clock in the morning, and his body was confused. He tumbled into bed, meditated vaguely on the probable presence of Sybille just a few air-minutes away in Zanzibar, and dropped into a sound sleep from which he awakened, what seemed like many hours later, to discover that it was still well before dawn.

He dawdled away the morning sightseeing in the old native quarter, hot and dusty, with unpaved streets and rows of tin shacks, and at midday returned to his hotel for a shower and lunch. Much the same national distribution in the restaurant—British, Japanese, Israeli—though the faces seemed different. He was on his second beer when Anthony Gracchus came in. The white hunter, broad-shouldered, pale, densely bearded, clad in khaki shorts, khaki shirt, seemed almost to have stepped out of the picture-cube Jijibhoi had once shown him. Instinctively Klein shrank back, turning toward the window, but too late: Gracchus had seen him. All chatter came to a halt in the restaurant as the dead man strode to Klein's table, pulled out a chair unasked, and seated himself; then, as though a motion picture projector had been halted and started again, the British engineers resumed their shouting, sounding somewhat strained now. "Small world," Gracchus said. "Crowded one, anyway. On your way to Zanzibar, are you, Klein?"

"In a day or so. Did you know I was here?"

"Of course not." Gracchus' harsh eyes twinkled slyly. "Sheer coincidence is what this is. She's there already."

"She is?"

"She and Zacharias and Mortimer. I hear you wiggled your way into Zion."

"Briefly," Klein said. "I saw Sybille. Briefly."

"Unsatisfactorily. So once again you've followed her here. Give it up, man. Give it up."

"I can't."

"*Can't!*" Gracchus scowled. "A neurotic's word, *can't*. What you mean is *won't*. A mature man can do anything he wants to that isn't a physical impossibility. Forget her. You're only annoying her, this way, interfering with her work, interfering with her—" Gracchus smiled. "With her life. She's been dead almost three years, hasn't she? Forget her. The world's full of other women. You're still young, you have money, you aren't ugly, you have professional standing—"

"Is this what you were sent here to tell me?"

"I wasn't sent here to tell you anything, friend. I'm only trying to save you from yourself. Don't go to Zanzibar. Go home and start your life again."

"When I saw her at Zion," Klein said, "she treated me with contempt. She amused herself at my expense. I want to ask her why she did that."

"Because you're a warm and she's a dead. To her, you're a clown. To all of us you're a clown. It's nothing personal, Klein. There's simply a gulf in attitudes, a gulf too wide for you to cross. You went to Zion drugged up like a Treasury man, didn't you? Pale face, bulgy eyes? You didn't fool anyone. You certainly didn't fool *her*. The game she played with you was her way of telling you that. Don't you know that?"

"I know it, yes."

"What more do you want, then? More humiliation?"

Klein shook his head wearily and stared at the tablecloth. After a moment he looked up, and his eyes met those of Gracchus, and he was astounded to realize that he trusted the hunter, that for the first time in his dealings with the deads he felt he was being met with sincerity. He said in a low voice, "We were very close, Sybille and I, and then she died, and now I'm nothing to her. I haven't been able to come to terms with that. I need her, still. I want to share my life with her, even now."

"But you can't."

"I know that. And still I can't help doing what I've been doing."

"There's only one thing you *can* share with her," Gracchus said. "That's your death. She won't descend to your level: you have to climb to hers."

"Don't be absurd."

"Who's absurd, me or you? Listen to me, Klein. I think you're a fool, I think you're a weakling, but I don't dislike you, I don't hold you to blame for your own foolishness. And so I'll help you, if you'll allow me." He reached into his breast pocket and withdrew a tiny metal tube with a safety catch at one end. "Do you know what this is?" Gracchus asked. "It's a self-defense dart, the kind all the women in New York carry. A good many deads carry them, too, because we never know when the reaction will start, when the mobs will turn against us. Only we don't use anesthetic drugs in ours. Listen, we can walk into any tavern in the native quarter and have a decent brawl going in five minutes, and in the confusion I'll put one of these darts into you, and we'll have you in Dar General Hospital fifteen minutes after that, crammed into a deep-freeze unit, and for a few thousand dollars we can ship you unthawed to California, and this time Friday night you'll be undergoing rekindling in, say, San Diego Cold Town. And when you come out of it you and Sybille will be on the same side of the gulf, do you see? If you're destined to get back together with her, ever, that's the only way. That way you have a chance. This way you have none."

"It's unthinkable," Klein said.

"Unacceptable, maybe. But not unthinkable. Nothing's unthinkable once somebody's thought it. You think it some more. Will you promise me that?

Think about it before you get aboard that plane for Zanzibar. I'll be staying here tonight and tomorrow, and then I'm going out to Arusha to meet some deads coming in for the hunting, and any time before then I'll do it for you if you say the word. Think about it. Will you think about it? Promise me that you'll think about it."

"I'll think about it," Klein said.

"Good. Good. Thank you. Now let's have lunch and change the subject. Do you like eating here?"

"One thing puzzles me. Why does this place have a clientele that's exclusively non-African? Does it dare to discriminate against blacks in a black republic?"

Gracchus laughed. "It's the blacks who discriminate, friend. This is considered a second-class hotel. All the blacks are at the Kilimanjaro or the Nyerere. Still, it's not such a bad place. I recommend the fish dishes, if you haven't tried them, and there's a decent white wine from Israel that—"

8.

O Lord, methought what pain it was to drown!
What dreadful noise of water in mine ears!
What sights of ugly death within mine eyes!
Methought I saw a thousand fearful wracks;
A thousand men that fishes gnawed upon;
Wedges of gold, great anchors, heaps of pearl,
Inestimable stones, unvalued jewels,
All scatt'red in the bottom of the sea.
Some lay in dead men's skulls, and in the
holes
Where eyes did once inhabit there were crept,
As 'twere in scorn of eyes, reflecting gems
That wooed the slimy bottom of the deep
And mocked the dead bones that lay scatt'red
by.

Shakespeare: Richard III

"—Israeli wine," Mick Dongan was saying. "Well, I'll try anything once, especially if there's some neat little irony attached to it. I mean, there we were in Egypt, in *Egypt*, at this fabulous dinner party in the hills at Luxor, and our host is a Saudi prince, no less, in full tribal costume right down to the sunglasses, and when they bring out the roast lamb he grins devilishly and says, Of course we could always drink Mouton-Rothschild, but I do happen to have a small stock of select Israeli wines in my cellar, and because I think you are, like myself, a connoisseur of small incongruities I've asked my steward to open a bottle or two of—Klein, do you see that girl who just come in?" It is January, 1981, early afternoon, a fine drizzle in the air. Klein is lunching with six colleagues from the history department of the Hanging Gardens atop the Westwood Plaza. The hotel is a huge ziggurat on stilts; the Hanging Gardens is a rooftop restaurant, ninety stories up, in freaky neo-Babylonian decor, all winged bulls and snorting dragons of blue and yellow tile, waiters with long curly beards and scimitars at their hips—gaudy nightclub by dark, campy faculty hangout by day. Klein looks to his left. Yes, a handsome woman, mid-twenties, coolly beautiful, serious-looking, taking a seat by herself, putting a stack of books and cassettes down on the table before her. Klein does not pick up strange girls: a matter of moral policy, and also a matter of innate shyness. Dongan teases him. "Go on over, will you? She's your type, I swear. Her eyes are the right color for you, aren't they?"

Klein has been complaining, lately, that there are too many blue-eyed girls in Southern California. Blue eyes are disturbing to him, somehow, even menacing. His own eyes are brown. So are hers: dark, warm, sparkling. He thinks he has seen her occasionally in the library. Perhaps they have even exchanged brief glances. "Go on," Dongan says. "Go *on*, Jorge. Go." Klein glares at him. He will not go. How can he intrude on this woman's privacy? To force himself on her—it would almost be like rape. Dongan smiles complacently; his bland grin is a merciless prod. Klein refuses to be stampeded. But then, as he hesitates, the girl smiles too, a quick shy smile, gone so soon he is not altogether sure it happened at all, but he is sure enough, and he finds himself rising, crossing the alabaster floor, hovering awkwardly over her, searching for some inspired words with which to make contact, and no words come, but still they make contact the old-fashioned way, eye to eye, and he is stunned by the intensity of what passes between them in that first implausible moment.

"Are you waiting for someone?" he mutters, stunned.

"No." The smile again, far less tentative. "Would you like to join me?"

She is a graduate student, he discovers quickly. Just got her master's, beginning now on her doctorate—the nineteenth-century East African slave trade, particular emphasis on Zanzibar. "How romantic," he says. "Zanzibar! Have you been there?"

"Never. I hope to go some day. Have you?"

"Not ever. But it always interested me, ever since I was a small boy collecting stamps. It was the last country in my album."

"Not in mine," she says. "Zululand was."

She knows him by name, it turns out. She had even been thinking of enrolling in his course on Nazism and Its Offspring. "Are you South American?" she asks.

"Born there. Raised here. My grandparents escaped to Buenos Aires in '37."

"Why Argentina? I thought that was a hotbed of Nazis."

"Was. Also full of German-speaking refugees, though. All their friends went there. But it was too unstable. My parents got out in '55, just before one of the big revolutions, and came to California. What about you?"

"British family. I was born in Seattle. My father's in the consular service. He—"

A waiter looms. They order sandwiches offhandedly. Lunch seems very unimportant now. The contact still holds. He sees Conrad's *Nostromo* in her stack of books; she is halfway through it, and he has just finished it, and the coincidence amuses them. Conrad is one of her favorites, she says. One of his, too. What about Faulkner? Yes, and Mann, and Virginia Woolf, and they share even a fondness for Hermann Broch, and a dislike for Hesse. How odd. Operas? *Freischütz, Holländer, Fidelio*, yes. "We have very Teutonic tastes," she observes. "We have very similar tastes," he adds. He finds himself holding her hand. "Amazingly similar," she says. Mick Dongan leers at him from the far side of the room; Klein gives him a terrible scowl. Dongan winks. "Let's get out of here," Klein says, just as she starts to say the same thing.

They talk half the night and make love until dawn. "You ought to know," he tells her solemnly over breakfast, "that I decided long ago never to get married and certainly never to have a child."

"So did I," she says. "When I was fifteen."

They were married four months later. Mick Dongan was his best man.

Gracchus said, as they left the restaurant, "You will think things over, won't you?"

"I will," Klein said. "I promise you that."

He went to his room, packed his suitcase, checked out, and took a cab to the airport, arriving in plenty of time for the afternoon flight to Zanzibar. The same melancholy little man was on duty as health officer when he landed, Barwani. "Sir, you have come back," Barwani said. "I thought you might. The other people have been here several days already."

"The other people?"

"When you were here last, sir, you kindly offered me a retainer in order that you might be informed when a certain person reached this island." Barwani's eyes gleamed. "That person, with two of her former companions, is here now."

Klein carefully placed a twenty-shilling note on the health officer's desk.

"At which hotel?"

Barwani's lips quirked. Evidently twenty shillings fell short of expectations. But Klein did not take out another banknote, and after a moment Barwani said, "As before. The Zanzibar House. And you, sir?"

"As before," Klein said. "I'll be staying at the Shirazi."

Sybille was in the garden of the hotel, going over that day's research notes, when the telephone call came from Barwani. "Don't let my papers blow away," she said to Zacharias, and went inside. When she returned, looking bothered, Zacharias said, "Is there trouble?"

She sighed. "Jorge. He's on his way to his hotel now."

"What a bore," Mortimer murmured. "I thought Gracchus might have brought him to his senses."

"Evidently not," Sybille said. "What are we going to do?"

"What would you like to do?" Zacharias asked.

She shook her head. "We can't allow this to go on, can we?"

The evening air was humid and fragrant. The long rains had come and gone, and the island was in the grip of the new season's lunatic fertility: outside the window of Klein's hotel room some vast twining vine was putting forth monstrous trumpet-shaped yellow flowers, and all about the hotel grounds everything was in blossom, everything was in a frenzy of moist young leaves. Klein's sensibility reverberated to that feeling of universal vigorous thrusting newness; he paced the room, full of energy, trying to devise some feasible stratagem. Go immediately to see Sybille? Force his way in, if necessary, with shouts and alarums, and demand to know why she had told him that fantastic tale of imaginary sultans? No. No. He would do no more confronting, no more lamenting; now that he was here, now that he was close by her, he would seek her out calmly, he would talk quietly, he would invoke memories of their old love, he would speak of Rilke and Woolf and Broch, of afternoons in Puerto Vallarta and nights in Santa Fe, of music heard and caresses shared, he would rekindle not their marriage, for that was impossible, but merely the remembrance of the bond that once had existed, he would win from her some acknowledgment of what had been, and then he would soberly and quietly exorcise that bond, he and she together, they would work to free him by speaking softly of the change that had come over their lives, until, after three hours or four or five, he had brought himself with her help to an acceptance of the unacceptable. That was all. He would demand nothing, he would beg for nothing, except only that she assist him for one evening in ridding his soul of this useless destructive obsession. Even a dead, even a capricious, wayward, volatile, whimsical, wanton dead, would surely see the desirability of that, and would freely give him her cooperation. Surely. And then home, and then new beginnings, too long postponed.

He made ready to go out.

There was a soft knock at the door. "Sir? Sir? You have visitors downstairs."

"Who?" Klein asked, though he knew the answer.

"A lady and two gentlemen," the bellhop replied. "The taxi has brought them from the Zanzibar House. They wait for you in the bar."

"Tell them I'll be down in a moment."

He went to the iced pitcher on the dresser, drank a glass of cold water mechanically, unthinkingly, poured himself a second, drained that too. This visit was unexpected; and why had she brought her entourage along? He had to struggle to regain that centeredness, that sense of purpose understood, which he thought he had attained before the knock. Eventually he left the room.

They were dressed crisply and impeccably this damp night, Zacharias in a tawny frock coat and pale green trousers, Mortimer in a belted white caftan trimmed with intricate brocade, Sybille in a simple lavender tunic. Their pale faces were unmarred by perspiration; they seemed perfectly composed, models of poise. No one sat near them in the bar. As Klein entered, they stood to greet him, but their smiles appeared sinister, having nothing of friendliness in them. Klein clung tight to his intended calmness. He said quietly, "It was kind of you to come. May I buy drinks for you?"

"We have ours already," Zacharias pointed out. "Let us be your hosts. What will you have?"

"Pimm's Number Six," Klein said. He tried to match their frosty smiles. "I admire your tunic, Sybille. You all look so debonair tonight that I feel shamed."

"You never were famous for your clothes," she said.

Zacharias returned from the counter with Klein's drink. He took it and toasted them gravely.

After a short while Klein said, "Do you think I could talk privately with you, Sybille?"

"There's nothing we have to say to one another that can't be said in front of Kent and Laurence."

"Nevertheless."

"I prefer not to, Jorge."

"As you wish." Klein peered straight into her eyes and saw nothing there, nothing, and flinched. All that he had meant to say fled his mind. Only churning fragments danced there; Rilke, Broch, Puerto Vallarta. He gulped at his drink.

Zacharias said, "We have a problem to discuss, Klein."

"Go on."

"The problem is you. You're causing great distress to Sybille. This is the second time, now, that you've followed her to Zanzibar, to the literal end of the earth, Klein, and you've made several attempts besides to enter a closed sanctuary in Utah under false pretenses, and this is interfering with Sybille's freedom, Klein, it's an impossible, intolerable interference."

"The deads are dead," Mortimer said. "We understand the depths of your feelings for your late wife, but this compulsive pursuit of her must be brought to an end."

"It will be," Klein said, staring at a point on the stucco wall midway between Zacharias and Sybille. "I want only an hour or two of private conversation with my—with Sybille, and then I promise you that there will be no further—"

"Just as you promised Anthony Gracchus," Mortimer said, "not to go to Zanzibar."

"I wanted—"

"We have our rights," said Zacharias. "We've gone through hell, literally through hell, to get where we are. You've infringed on our right to be left alone. You bother us. You bore us. You annoy us. We hate to be annoyed." He looked toward Sybille. She nodded. Zacharias' hand vanished into the breast pocket of his coat. Mortimer seized Klein's wrist with astonishing suddenness and jerked his arm forward. A minute metal tube glistened in Zacharias' huge fist. Klein had seen such a tube in the hand of Anthony Gracchus only the day before.

"No," Klein gasped. "I don't believe—*no!*"

Zacharias plunged the cold tip of the tube quickly into Klein's forearm.

"The freezer unit is coming," Mortimer said. "It'll be here in five minutes or less."

"What if it's late?" Sybille asked anxiously. "What if something irreversible happens to his brain before it gets here?"

"He's not even entirely dead yet," Zacharias reminded her. "There's time. There's ample time. I spoke to the doctor myself, a very intelligent Chinese, flawless command of English. He was most sympathetic. They'll have him frozen within a couple of minutes of death. We'll book cargo passage aboard the morning plane for Dar. He'll be in the United States within twenty-four hours, I guarantee that. San Diego will be notified. Everything will be all right, Sybille!"

Jorge Klein lay slumped across the table. The bar had emptied the moment he had cried out and lurched forward: the half-dozen customers had fled, not caring to mar their holidays by sharing an evening with the presence of death, and the waiters and bartenders, big-eyed, terrified, lurked in the hallway. A heart attack, Zacharias had announced, some kind of sudden attack, maybe a stroke, where's the telephone? No one had seen the tiny tube do its work.

Sybille trembled. "If anything goes wrong—"

"I hear the sirens now," Zacharias said.

From his desk at the airport Daud Mahmoud Barwani watched the bulky refrigerated coffin being loaded by grunting porters aboard the morning plane for Dar. And then, and then, and then? They would ship the dead man to the far side of the world, to America, and breathe new life into him, and he would go once more among men. Barwani shook his head. These people! The man who was alive is now dead, and these dead ones, who knows what they are? Who knows? Best that the dead remain dead, as was intended in the time of first things. Who could have foreseen a day when the dead returned from the grave? Not I. And who can foresee what we will all become, a hundred years from now? Not I. Not I. A hundred years from now I will sleep, Barwani thought. I will sleep, and it will not matter to me at all what sort of creatures walk the earth.

9.

We die with the dying:
See, they depart, and we go with them.
We are born with the dead:
See, they return, and bring us with them.
T. S. Eliot: Little Gidding

On the day of his awakening he saw no one except the attendants at the rekindling house, who bathed him and fed him and helped him to walk slowly around his room. They said nothing to him, nor he to them; words seemed irrelevant. He felt strange in his skin, too snugly contained, as though all his life he had worn ill-fitting clothes and now had for the first time encountered a competent tailor. The images that his eyes brought him were sharp, unnaturally clear, and faintly haloed by prismatic colors, an effect that imperceptibly vanished as the day passed. On the second day he was visited by the San Diego Guidefather, not at all the formidable patriarch he had imagined, but rather a cool efficient executive, about fifty years old, who greeted him cordially and told him briefly of the disciplines and routines he must master before he could leave the Cold Town. "What month is this?" Klein asked, and Guidefather told him it was June, the seventeenth of June, 1993. He had slept four weeks.

Now it is the morning of the third day after his awakening, and he has guests: Sybille, Nerita, Zacharias, Mortimer, Gracchus. They file into his room and stand in an arc at the foot of his bed, radiant in the glow of light that pierces the narrow windows. Like demigods, like angels, glittering with a dazzling inward brilliance, and now he is of their company. Formally they embrace him, first Gracchus, then Nerita, then Mortimer. Zacharias advances next to his bedside, Zacharias who sent him into death, and he smiles at Klein and Klein returns the smile, and they embrace. Then it is Sybille's turn: she slips her hand between his, he draws her close, her lips brush his cheek, his touch hers, his arm encircles her shoulders.

"Hello," she whispers.

"Hello," he says.

They ask him how he feels, how quickly his strength is returning, whether he has been out of bed yet, how soon he will commence his drying-off. The style of their conversation is the oblique, elliptical style favored by the deads, but not nearly so clipped and cryptic as the way of speech they normally would use among themselves; they are favoring him, leading him inch by inch into their customs. Within five minutes he thinks he is getting the knack.

He says, using their verbal shorthand, "I must have been a great burden to you."

"You were, you were," Zacharias agrees. "But all that is done with now."

"We forgive you," Mortimer says.

"We welcome you among us," declares Sybille.

They talk about their plans for the months ahead. Sybille is nearly finished with her work on Zanzibar; she will retreat to Zion Cold Town for the summer months to write her thesis. Mortimer and Nerita are off to Mexico to tour the ancient temples and pyramids; Zacharias is going to Ohio, to his beloved mounds. In the autumn they will reassemble at Zion and plan the winter's amusement: a tour of Egypt, perhaps, or Peru, the heights of Machu Picchu. Ruins, archeological sites, delight them; in the places where death has been busiest, their joy is most intense. They are flushed, excited, verbose—virtually chattering, now. Away we will go, to Zimbabwe, to Palenque, to Angkor, to Knossos, to Uxmal, to Nineveh, to Mohenjodaro. And as they go on and on, talking with hands and eyes and smiles and even words, even words, torrents of words, they blur and become unreal to him, they are mere dancing puppets jerking about a badly painted stage, they are droning insects, wasps or bees or mosquitoes, with all their talk of travels and festivals, of Boghazköy and Babylon, of Megiddo and Masada, and he ceases to hear them, he tunes them out, he lies there smiling, eyes glazed, mind adrift. It perplexes him that he has so little interest in them. But then he realizes that it is a mark of his liberation. He is freed of old chains now. Will he join their set? Why should he? Perhaps he will travel with them, perhaps not, as the whim takes him. More likely not. Almost certainly not. He does not need their company. He has his own interests. He will follow Sybille about no longer. He does not need, he does not want, he will not seek. Why should he become one of them, rootless, an amoral wanderer, a ghost made flesh? Why should he embrace the values and customs of these people who had given him to death as dispassionately as they might swat an insect, only because he had bored them, because he had annoyed them? He does not hate them for what they did to him, he feels no resentment that he can identify, he merely chooses to detach himself from them. Let them float on from ruin to ruin, let them pursue death from continent to continent; he will go his own way. Now that he has crossed the interface he finds that Sybille no longer matters to him.

—Oh, sir, things change—

"We'll go now," Sybille says softly.

He nods. He makes no other reply.

"We'll see you after your drying-off," Zacharias tells him, and touches him slightly with his knuckles, a farewell gesture used only by the deads.

"See you," Mortimer says.

"See you," says Gracchus.

"Soon," Nerita says.

Never, Klein says, saying it without words, but so they will understand. Never. Never. Never. I will never see any of you. I will never see you, Sybille. The syllables echo through his brain, and the word, *never, never, never*, rolls over him like the breaking surf, cleansing him, purifying him, healing him. He is free. He is alone.

"Goodbye," Sybille calls from the hallway.

"Goodbye," he says.

It was years before he saw her again. But they spent the last days of '99 together, shooting dodos under the shadow of mighty Kilimanjaro.

THE ALIENS ARE HERE!

Mrs. Grendon looked doubtful. Then her eye seemed to catch a movement. She looked fixedly to one side. "Here come one now, the female one," she said.

Gregory turned to look where she did. Nothing was visible. His mouth was dry. "How many are there, Mrs. Grendon?"

Then he saw the short grass stir, flatten, and raise near at hand, and let out a cry of alarm. Wrenching off his riding boot, he swung it in an arc, low above the ground. It struck something concealed in thin air. Almost at once, he received a terrific kick in the thigh, and fell backwards. Despite the hurt, fear made him jump up almost at once.

Mrs. Grendon was changing. Her mouth collapsed as if it would run off one corner of her face. Her head sagged to one side. Her shoulders fell. A deep crimson blush momentarily suffused her features, then drained, and as it drained she dwindled like a deflated rubber balloon. Gregory sank to his knees, whimpering, buried his face in his hands and pressed his hands to the grass. Darkness overcame him.

BRIAN W. ALDISS

THE SALIVA TREE

TOR®
A TOM DOHERTY ASSOCIATES BOOK
NEW YORK

THE SALIVA TREE

A TOR Book
Published by Tom Doherty Associates, Inc.
49 West 24 Street
New York, NY 10010

ISBN: 0-812-55952-5 Can. ISBN: 0-812-55955-3

Library of Congress Catalog Card Number: 88-50634

First edition: December 1988

Printed in the United States of America

0 9 8 7 6 5 4 3 2 1

There is neither speech nor language:
but their voices are heard among them.
PSALM XIX

"You know, I'm really much exercised about the Fourth Dimension," said the fair-haired young man, with a suitable earnestness in his voice.

"Um," said his companion, staring up at the night sky.

"It seems very much in evidence these days. Do you not think you catch a glimpse of it in the drawings of Aubrey Beardsley?"

"Um," said his companion.

They stood together on a low rise to the east of the sleepy East Anglian town of Cottersall, watching the stars, shivering a little in the chill February air. They are both young men in their early twenties. The one who is occupied with the Fourth Dimension is called Bruce Fox; he is tall and fair, and works as junior clerk in the Norwich firm of lawyers, Prendergast and Tout. The other, who has so far vouchsafed us only an *um* or two, although he is to figure largely as the hero of our account, is by name Gregory Rolles. He is tall and dark, with grey eyes set in his handsome and intelligent face. He and Fox have sworn to

Think Large, thus distinguishing themselves, at least in their own minds, from all the rest of the occupants of Cottersall in these last years of the nineteenth century.

"There's another!" exclaimed Gregory, breaking at last from the realm of monosyllables. He pointed a gloved finger up at the constellation of Auriga the Charioteer. A meteor streaked across the sky like a runaway flake of the Milky Way, and died in mid-air.

"Beautiful!" they said together.

"It's funny," Fox said, prefacing his words with an oft-used phrase, "the stars and men's minds are so linked together and always have been, even in the centuries of ignorance before Charles Darwin. They always seem to play an ill-defined role in man's affairs. They help me think large too, don't they you, Greg?"

"You know what I think—I think that some of those stars may be occupied. By people, I mean." He breathed heavily, overcome by what he was saying. "People who—perhaps they are better than us, live in a just society, wonderful people . . ."

"I know, Socialists to a man!" Fox exclaimed. This was one point on which he did not share his friend's advanced thinking. He had listened to Mr. Tout talking in the office, and thought he knew better than his rich friend how these socialists, of which one heard so much these days, were undermining society. "Stars full of socialists!"

"Better than stars full of Christians! Why, if the stars were full of Christians, no doubt they would already have sent missionaries down here to preach their Gospel."

"I wonder if there ever will be planetary journeys as predicted by Nunsowe Greene and Monsieur Jules Verne—" Fox said, when the appearance of a fresh meteor stopped him in mid-sentence.

Like the last, this meteor seemed to come from the

general direction of Auriga. It travelled slowly, and it glowed red, and it sailed grandly towards them. They both exclaimed at once, and gripped each other by the arm. The magnificent spark burned in the sky, larger now, so that its red aura appeared to encase a brighter orange glow. It passed overhead (afterwards, they argued whether it had not made a slight noise as it passed), and disappeared below a clump of willow. They knew it had been near. For an instant, the land had shone with its light.

Gregory was the first to break the silence.

"Bruce, Bruce, did you see that? That was no ordinary fireball!"

"It was so big! What was it?"

"Perhaps our heavenly visitor has come at last!"

"Hey, Greg, it must have landed by your friends' farm—the Grendon place—mustn't it?"

"You're right! I must pay old Mr. Grendon a visit tomorrow and see if he or his family saw anything of this."

They talked excitedly, stamping their feet as they exercised their lungs. Their conversation was the conversation of optimistic young men, and included much speculative matter that began "Wouldn't it be wonderful if—", or "Just supposing—". Then they stopped and laughed at their own absurd beliefs.

"It must be nearly nine o'clock," Fox said at last. "I didn't mean to be so late tonight. It's funny how fast time passes. We'd best be getting back, Greg."

They had brought no lantern, since the night was both clear and dry. It was but two miles by the track back to the outlying houses of Cottersall. They stepped it out lustily, arm linked in arm in case one of them tripped in cart ruts, for Fox had to be up at five in the morning if he was to bicycle to his work punctually. The little village lay silent, or almost so. In the baker's house where Gregory lodged, a gaslight burned and a piano could be heard. As they

halted smartly at the side door, Fox said slyly, "So you'll be seeing all the Grendon family tomorrow?"

"It seems probable, unless that red hot planetary ship has already borne them off to a better world."

"Tell us true, Greg—you really go to see that pretty Nancy Grendon, don't you?"

Gregory struck his friend playfully on the shoulder.

"No need for your jealousy, Bruce! I go to see the father, not the daughter. Though the one is female, the other is progressive and that must interest me more just yet. Nancy has beauty, true, but her father—ah, her father has electricity!"

Laughing, they cheerfully shook hands and parted for the night.

On Grendon's farm, things were a deal less tranquil, as Gregory was to discover.

Gregory Rolles rose before seven next morning as was his custom. It was while he was lighting his gas mantle, and wishing the baker would install electricity, that a swift train of thought led him to reflect again on the phenomenal thing in the previous night's sky. Mrs. Fenn, the baker's wife, who had already lit his fire, brought him up hot water for washing and scalding water for shaving and, later, a mighty tray full of breakfast. Throughout this activity, and indeed while he ate his porridge and chops, Gregory remained abstracted, letting his mind wander luxuriously over all the possibilities that the "meteor" illuminated. He decided that he would ride out to see Mr. Grendon within the hour.

He was lucky in being able, at this stage in his life, to please himself largely as to how his days were spent, for his father was a person of some substance. Edward Rolles had had the fortune, at the time of the Crimean War, to meet Escoffier, and with some help from the great chef had brought onto the market

a baking powder, "Eugenol", that, being slightly more palatable and less deleterious to the human system than its rivals, had achieved great commercial success. As a result, Gregory had attended one of the Cambridge colleges.

Now, having gained a degree, he was poised on the verge of a career. But which career? He had acquired—more as a result of his intercourse with other students than with those officially deputed to instruct him—some understanding of the sciences; his essays had been praised and some of his poetry published, so that he inclined towards literature; and an uneasy sense that life for everyone outside the privileged classes contained too large a proportion of misery led him to think seriously of a political career. In Divinity, too, he was well-grounded; but at least the idea of Holy Orders did not tempt him.

While he wrestled with his future, he undertook to live away from home, since his relations with his father were never smooth. By rusticating himself in the heart of East Anglia, he hoped to gather material for a volume tentatively entitled "Wanderings with a Socialist Naturalist", which would assuage all sides of his ambitions. Nancy Grendon, who had a pretty hand with a pencil, might even execute a little emblem for the title page . . . Perhaps he might be permitted to dedicate it to his author friend, Mr. Herbert George Wells . . .

He dressed himself warmly, for the morning was cold as well as dull, and went down to the baker's stables. When he had saddled his mare, Daisy, he swung himself up and set out along a road that the horse knew well.

The sun had been up for something over an hour, yet the sky and the landscape were drab in the extreme. Two sorts of East Anglian landscape met here, trapped by the confused wanderings of the River Oast: the unfarmable heathland and the

unfarmable fen. There were few trees, and those stunted, so that the four fine elms that stood on one side of the Grendon farm made a cynosure for miles around.

The land rose slightly towards the farm, the area about the house forming something of a little island amid marshy ground and irregular stretches of water that gave back to the sky its own dun tone. The gate over the little bridge was, as always, open wide; Daisy picked her way through the mud to the stables, where Gregory left her to champ oats contentedly. Cuff and her pup, Lardie, barked loudly about Gregory's heels as usual, and he patted their heads on his way over to the house.

Nancy came hurrying out to meet him before he got to the front door.

"We had some excitement last night, Gregory," she said. He noted with pleasure she had at last brought herself to use his first name.

"Something bright and glaring!" she said. "I was retiring, when this noise come and then this light, and I rush to look out through the curtains, and there's this here great thing like an egg sinking into our pond." In her speech, and particularly when she was excited, she carried the lilting accent of Norfolk.

"The meteor!" Gregory exclaimed. "Bruce Fox and I were out last night as we were the night before, watching for the lovely Aurigids that arrive every February, when we saw an extra big one. I said then it was coming over very near here."

"Why, it almost landed on our house," Nancy said. She looked very pleasing this morning, with her lips red, her cheeks shining, and her chestnut curls all astray. As she spoke, her mother appeared in apron and cap, with a wrap hurriedly thrown over her shoulders.

"Nancy, you come in, standing freezing like that! You ent daft, girl, are you? Hello, Gregory, how be

going on? I didn't reckon as we'd see you today. Come in and warm yourself."

"Good-day to you, Mrs. Grendon. I'm hearing about your wonderful meteor of last night."

"It was a falling star, according to Bert Neckland. I ent sure what it was, but it certainly stirred up the animals, that I *do* know."

"Can you see anything of it in the pond?" Gregory asked.

"Let me show you," Nancy said.

Mrs. Grendon returned indoors. She went slowly and grandly, her back very straight and an unaccustomed load before her. Nancy was her only daughter; there was a younger son, Archie, a stubborn lad who had fallen at odds with his father and now was apprenticed to a blacksmith in Norwich; and no other children living. Three infants had not survived the mixture of fogs alternating with bitter east winds that comprised the typical Cottersall winter. But now the farmer's wife was unexpectedly gravid again, and would bear her husband another baby when the spring came in.

As Nancy led Gregory over to the pond, he saw Grendon with his two labourers working in the West Field, but they did not wave.

"Was your father not excited by the arrival last night?"

"That he was—when it happened! He went out with his shot gun, and Bert Neckland with him. But there was nothing to see but bubbles in the pond and steam over it, and this morning he wouldn't discuss it, and said that work must go on whatever happen."

They stood beside the pond, a dark and extensive slab of water with rushes on the farther bank and open country beyond. As they looked at its ruffled surface, they stood with the windmill black and bulky on their left hand. It was to this that Nancy now pointed.

Mud had been splashed across the boards high up the sides of the mill; some was to be seen even on the tip of the nearest white sail. Gregory surveyed it all with interest. Nancy, however, was still pursuing her own line of thought.

"Don't you reckon Father works too hard, Gregory? When he ent outside doing jobs, he's in reading his pamphlets and his electricity manuals. He never rests but when he sleeps."

"Um. Whatever went into the pond went in with a great smack! There's no sign of anything there now, is there? Not that you can see an inch below the surface."

"You being a friend of his, Mum thought perhaps as you'd say something to him. He don't go to bed till ever so late—sometimes it's near midnight, and then he's up again at three and a half o'clock. Would you speak to him? You know Mother dassent."

"Nancy, we ought to see whatever it was that went in the pond. It can't have dissolved. How deep is the water? Is it very deep?"

"Oh, you aren't listening, Gregory Rolles! Bother the old meteor!"

"This is a matter of science, Nancy. Don't you see—"

"Oh, rotten old science, is it? Then I don't want to hear. I'm cold, standing out here. You can have a good look if you like, but I'm going in before I gets froze. It was only an old stone out of the sky, because I heard Father and Bert Neckland agree to it."

"Fat lot Bert Neckland knows about such things!" he called to her departing back. She had the prettiest ringlets on her neck, but really he didn't want to get involved with a nineteen-year-old farmer's daughter. It was a pity more girls didn't believe in Free Love, as did most of his male acquaintances.

He looked down at the dark water. Whatever it *was* that had arrived last night, it was here, only a

few feet from him. He longed to discover what remained of it. Vivid pictures entered his mind: his name in headlines in "The Morning Post", the Royal Society making him an honorary member, his father embracing him and pressing him to return home.

Thoughtfully, he walked over to the barn. Hens ran clucking out of his way as he entered and stood looking up, waiting for his eyes to adjust to the dim light. There, as he remembered it, was a little rowing boat. Perhaps in his courting days old Mr. Grendon had taken his prospective wife out for excursions on the Oast in it. Surely it had not been used in years.

He moved the long ladder over to climb and inspect it, and a cat went flying across the rafters in retreat. The inside of the boat was filthy, but two oars lay there, and it seemed intact. The craft had been hitched to its present position by two ropes thrown over a higher beam; it was a simple enough matter to lower it to the ground.

At that point, Gregory had a moment of prudence for other people's property. He went into the farm and asked Mrs. Grendon if he might embark on the pond with it. That complaisant lady said he might do as he wished, and accordingly he dragged the boat from the barn and launched it in the shallows of the pond. It floated. The boards had dried, and water leaked through a couple of seams, but not nearly enough to deter him. Climbing delicately in among the straw and filth, he pushed off.

From here, the farm, or such of it as he could see, presented a somewhat sinister aspect. The mill loomed above him, dismal and tarred black, only its sails white and creaking in the slight wind. To his other side, the blank-faced end of the barn looked immense and meaningless. Behind it he could see the backs of cowsheds with, beyond them, the raw new brick of the back of Grendon's machine house,

where he made electricity. Between barn and mill, he could see the farmhouse, but the upper storey only, because of the lie of the land. Its decrepit humps of thatch and the tall stack of its chimney gave it a forbidding air. He mused on the strangeness that overcame one from looking at human works from an angle from which they were never designed to be seen, and wondered if there were similar angles in nature. Presumably there were, for behind him where the pond ended were only ragged willows topping reed beds. It looked as if there should have been something else—a little land at least—but no land showed, only the willows and the watery sky.

Now he was over the approximate centre of the pond. He shipped his oars and peered over the side. There was an agitation in the water, and nothing could be seen, although he imagined much.

As he stared over the one side, the boat unexpectedly tipped to the other. Gregory swung round. The boat listed heavily to the left, so that the oars rolled over that way. He could see nothing. Yet—he heard something. It was a sound much like a hound slowly panting. And whatever made it was about to capsize the boat.

"What is it?" he said, as all the skin pricked up his back and skull.

The boat lurched, for all the world as if someone invisible were trying to get into it. Frightened, he grasped the oar, and, without thinking, swept it over that side of the rowing boat.

It struck something solid where there was only air.

Dropping the oar in surprise, he put out his hand. It touched something yielding. At the same time, his arm was violently struck.

His actions were then entirely governed by instinct. Thought did not enter the matter. He picked up the oar again and smote the thin air with it. It hit something. There was a splash, and the boat righted

itself so suddenly he was almost pitched into the water. Even while it still rocked, he was rowing frantically for the shallows, dragging the boat from the water, and running for the safety of the farmhouse.

Only at the door did he pause. His reason returned, his heart began gradually to stop stammering its fright. He stood looking at the seamed wood of the porch, trying to evaluate what he had seen and what had actually happened. But what had happened?

Forcing himself to go back to the pond, he stood by the boat and looked across the sullen face of the water. It lay undisturbed, except by surface ripples. He looked at the boat. A quantity of water lay in the bottom of it. He thought, all that happened was that I nearly capsized, and I let my idiot fears run away with me. Shaking his head, he pulled the boat back to the barn.

Gregory, as he often did, stayed to eat lunch at the farm, but he saw nothing of the farmer till milking time.

Joseph Grendon was in his late forties, and a few years senior to his wife. He had a gaunt solemn face and a heavy beard that made him look older than he was. For all his seriousness, he greeted Gregory civilly enough. They stood together in the gathering dusk as the cows swung behind them into their regular stalls. Together they walked into the machine house next door, and Grendon lit the oil burners that started the steam engine into motion that would turn the generator that would supply the vital spark.

"I smell the future in here," Gregory said, smiling. By now, he had forgotten the shock of the morning.

"The future will have to get on without me. I shall be dead by then." The farmer spoke as he walked, putting each word reliably before the next.

"That is what you always say. You're wrong—the future is rushing upon us."

"You ent far wrong there, Master Gregory, but I won't have no part of it, I reckon. I'm an old man now. Do you know what I was reading in one of those London papers last night? They do say as how before another half-century is out every house in the country will be supplied with electrical lighting from one big central power house in London. This here old machine won't be no good then, will it?"

"It will be the end of the gas industry, that's for sure. That will cause much unemployment."

"Well, of course, in remote districts like this here primitive place, you wouldn't get gas in a dozen centuries. But electrical lighting is easier to conduct from one place to another than gas is. Here she come!"

This last exclamation was directed at a flicker of light in the pilot bulb overhead. They stood there contemplating with satisfaction the wonderful machinery. As steam pressure rose, the great leather belt turned faster and faster, and the flicker in the pilot bulb grew stronger. Although Gregory was used to a home lit by both gas and electricity, he never felt the excitement of it as he did here, out in the wilds, where the nearest incandescent bulb was probably in Norwich, a great part of a day's journey away.

"Why did you really decide to have this plant built, Joseph?"

"Like I told you, it's safer than lanterns in the sheds and the sties and anywhere with dry straw about the place. My father had a bad fire here when I was a boy that put the wind up me proper . . . Did I ever tell you as how Bert Neckland's older brother used to work for me once, till I got this here equipment in? He was a regular Bible-thumper, he was, and do you know what he told me? He said as how this here electrical lighting was too bright and

devilish to be God's work, and in consequence he refused to let it shine on him. So I told him, I said, Well, I ent having you going round with an umbrella up all hours of darkness, and I gave him his wages and I tell him to clear off out if that's the way he feels."

"And he did?"

"He ent been back here since."

"Idiot! All things are possible now. The Steam Age was wonderful in its way, or must have seemed so to the people that lived in it, but in this new Electric Age—anything's possible. Do you know what I believe, Joseph? I believe that before so very many years are up, we shall have electrical flying machines. Who knows, we may even be able to make them big enough to fly to the moon! Oh, I tell you, I just cannot wait till the New Century. By then, who knows, all men may be united in brotherhood, and then we shall see some progress."

"I don't know. I shall be united in my grave by then."

"Nonsense, you can live to be a hundred."

Now a pale flickering radiance illuminated the room. By contrast, everything outside looked black. Grendon nodded in satisfaction, made some adjustments to the burners, and they went outside.

Free from the bustle of the steam engine, they could hear the noise the cows were making. At milking time, the animals were usually quiet; something had upset them. The farmer ran quickly into the milking shed, with Gregory on his heels.

The new light, radiating from a bulb hanging above the stalls, showed the beasts of restless demeanour and rolling eye. Bert Neckland stood as far away from the door as possible, grasping his stick and letting his mouth hang open.

"What in blazes you staring at, bor?" Grendon asked.

Neckland slowly shut his mouth.

"We had a scare," he said. "Something come in here," he said.

"Did you see what it was?" Gregory asked.

"No, there weren't nothing to see. It was a ghost, that's what it was. It come right in here and touched the cows. It touched me too. It was a ghost."

The farmer snorted. "A tramp more like. You couldn't see because the light wasn't on."

His man shook his head emphatically. "Light weren't that bad. I tell you, whatever it was, it come right up to me and touched me." He stopped, and pointed to the edge of the stall. "Look there! See, I weren't telling you no lie, master. It was a ghost, and there's its wet hand-print."

They crowded round and examined the worn and chewed timber at the corner of the partition between two stalls. An indefinite patch of moisture darkened the wood. Gregory's thoughts went back to his experience on the pond, and again he felt the prickle of unease along his spine. But the farmer said stoutly "Nonsense, it's a bit of cowslime. Now you get on with the milking, Bert, and let's have no more hossing about, because I want my tea. Where's Cuff?"

Bert looked defiant.

"If you don't believe me, maybe you'll believe the bitch. She saw whatever it was and went for it. It kicked her over, but she ran it out of here."

"I'll see if I can see her," Gregory said.

He ran outside and began calling the bitch. By now it was almost entirely dark. He could see nothing in the wide space of the front yard, and so set off in the other direction, down the path towards the pig sties and the fields, calling Cuff as he went. He paused. Low and savage growls sounded ahead, under the elm trees. It was Cuff. He went slowly forward. At this moment, he cursed that electric light meant lack of lanterns, and wished too that he had a weapon.

"Who's there?" he called.

The farmer came up by his side. "Let's charge 'em!"

They ran forward. The trunks of the four great elms were clear against the western sky, with water glinting leadenly behind them. The dog became visible. As Gregory saw Cuff, she sailed into the air, whirled round, and flew at the farmer. He flung up his arms and warded off the body. At the same time, Gregory felt a rush of air as if someone unseen had run past him, and a stale muddy smell filled his nostrils. Staggering, he looked behind him. The wan light from the cowsheds spread across the path between the outhouses and the farmhouse. Beyond the light, more distantly, was the silent countryside behind the grain store. Nothing untoward could be seen.

"They killed my old Cuff," said the farmer.

Gregory knelt down beside him to look at the bitch. There was no mark of injury on her, but she was dead, her fine head lying limp.

"She knew there was something there," Gregory said. "She went to attack whatever it was and it got her first. What was it? Whatever in the world was it?"

"They killed my old Cuff," said the farmer again, unhearing. He picked the body up in his arms, turned, and carried it towards the house. Gregory stood where he was, mind and heart equally uneasy.

He jumped violently when a step sounded nearby. It was Bert Neckland.

"What, did that there ghost kill the old bitch?" he asked.

"It killed the bitch certainly, but it was something more terrible than a ghost."

"That's one of them ghosts, bor. I seen plenty in my time. I ent afraid of ghosts, are you?"

"You looked fairly sick in the cowshed a minute ago."

The farmhand put his fists on his hips. He was no more than a couple of years older than Gregory, a stocky young man with a spotty complexion and a snub nose that gave him at once an air of comedy and menace. "Is that so, Master Gregory? Well, you looks pretty funky standing there now."

"I am scared. I don't mind admitting it. But only because we have something here a lot nastier than any spectre."

Neckland came a little closer.

"Then if you are so blooming windy, perhaps you'll be staying away from the farm in future."

"Certainly not." He tried to edge back into the light, but the labourer got in his way.

"If I was you, I should stay away." He emphasized his point by digging an elbow into Gregory's coat. "And just remember that Nancy was interested in me long afore you come along, bor."

"Oh, that's it, is it! I think Nancy can decide for herself in whom she is interested, don't you?"

"I'm *telling* you who she's interested in, see? And mind you don't forget, see?" He emphasized the words with another nudge. Gregory pushed his arm away angrily. Neckland shrugged his shoulders and walked off. As he went, he said, "You're going to get worse than ghosts if you keep hanging round here."

Gregory was shaken. The suppressed violence in the man's voice suggested that he had been harbouring malice for some time. Unsuspectingly, Gregory had always gone out of his way to be cordial, had regarded the sullenness as mere slow-wittedness and done his socialist best to overcome the barrier between them. He thought of following Neckland and trying to make up with him; but that would look too feeble. Instead, he followed the way the farmer had gone with his dead bitch, and made for the house.

* * *

Gregory Rolles was too late back to Cottersall that night to meet his friend Fox. The next night, the weather became exceedingly chilly and Gabriel Woodcock, the oldest inhabitant, was prophesying snow before the winter was out (a not very venturesome prophecy to be fulfilled within forty-eight hours, thus impressing most of the inhabitants of the village, for they took pleasure in being impressed and exclaiming and saying "Well I never!" to each other). The two friends met in "The Wayfarer", where the fires were bigger, though the ale was weaker, than in the "Three Poachers" at the other end of the village.

Seeing to it that nothing dramatic was missed from his account, Gregory related the affairs of the previous day, omitting any reference to Neckland's pugnacity. Fox listened fascinated, neglecting both his pipe and his ale.

"So you see how it is, Bruce," Gregory concluded. "In that deep pond by the mill lurks a vehicle of some sort, the very one we saw in the sky, and in it lives an invisible being of evil intent. You see how I fear for my friends there. Should I tell the police about it, do you think?"

"I'm sure it would not help the Grendons to have old Farrish bumping out there on his penny-farthing," Fox said, referring to the local representative of the law. He took a long draw first on the pipe and then on the glass. "But I'm not sure you have your conclusions quite right, Greg. Understand, I don't doubt the facts, amazing though they are. I mean, we were more or less expecting celestial visitants. The world's recent blossoming with gas and electricity lighting in its cities at night must have been a signal to half the nations of space that we are now civilized down here. But have our visitants done any deliberate harm to anyone?"

"They nearly drowned me and they killed poor

Cuff. I don't see what you're getting at. They haven't begun in a very friendly fashion, have they now?"

"Think what the situation must seem like to them. Suppose they come from Mars or the Moon—we know their world must be absolutely different from Earth. They may be terrified. And it can hardly be called an unfriendly act to try to get into your rowing boat. The first unfriendly act was yours, when you struck out with the oar."

Gregory bit his lip. His friend had a point. "I was scared."

"It may have been because they were scared that they killed Cuff. The dog attacked them, after all, didn't she? I feel sorry for these creatures, alone in an unfriendly world."

"You keep saying 'these'! As far as we know, there is only one of them."

"My point is this, Greg. You have completely gone back on your previous enlightened attitude. You are all for killing these poor things instead of trying to speak to them. Remember what you were saying about other worlds being full of socialists? Try thinking of these chaps as invisible socialists and see if that doesn't make them easier to deal with."

Gregory fell to stroking his chin. Inwardly, he acknowledged that Bruce Fox's words made a great impression on him. He had allowed panic to prejudice his judgement; as a result, he had behaved as immoderately as a savage in some remote corner of the Empire confronted by his first steam locomotive.

"I'd better get back to the farm and sort things out as soon as possible," he said. "If these things really do need help, I'll help them."

"That's it. But try not to think of them as 'things'. Think of them as—as—I know, as The Aurigans."

"Aurigans it is. But don't be so smug, Bruce. If you'd been in that boat—"

"I know, old friend. I'd have died of fright." To this monument of tact, Fox added, "Do as you say, go back and sort things out as soon as possible. I'm longing for the next instalment of this mystery. It's quite the jolliest thing since Sherlock Holmes."

Gregory Rolles went back to the farm. But the sorting out of which Bruce had spoken took longer than he expected. This was chiefly because the Aurigans seemed to have settled quietly into their new home after the initial day's troubles.

They came forth no more from the pond, as far as he could discover; at least they caused no more disturbance. The young graduate particularly regretted this since he had taken his friend's words much to heart, and wanted to prove how enlightened and benevolent he was towards this strange form of life. After some days, he came to believe the Aurigans must have left as unexpectedly as they arrived. Then a minor incident convinced him otherwise; and that same night, in his snug room over the baker's shop, he described it to his correspondent in Worcester Park, Surrey.

> *Dear Mr. Wells,*
>
> *I must apologize for my failure to write earlier, owing to lack of news concerning the Grendon Farm affair.*
>
> *Only today, the Aurigans showed themselves again!—if indeed "showed" is the right word for invisible creatures.*
>
> *Nancy Grendon and I were in the orchard feeding the hens. There is still much snow lying about, and everywhere is very white. As the poultry came running to Nancy's tub, I saw a disturbance further down the orchard—merely some snow dropping from an apple bough, but the*

movement caught my eye, and I then saw a procession *of falling snow proceed towards us from tree to tree. The grass is long there, and I soon noted the stalks being thrust aside by* an unknown agency! *I directed Nancy's attention to the phenomenon. The motion in the grass stopped only a few yards from us.*

Nancy was startled, but I determined to acquit myself more like a Briton than I had previously. Accordingly, I advanced and said, "Who are you? What do you want? We are your friends if you are friendly."

No answer came. I stepped forward again, and now the grass again fell back, and I could see by the way it was pressed down that the creature must have large feet. By the movement of the grasses, I could see he was running. I cried to him and ran too. He went round the side of the house, and then over the frozen mud in the farmyard I could see no further trace of him. But instinct led me forward, past the barn to the pond.

Surely enough, I then saw the cold, muddy water rise and heave, as if engulfing a body that slid quietly in. Shards of broken ice were thrust aside, and by an outward motion, I could see where the strange being went. In a flurry and a small whirlpool, he was gone, and I have no doubt dived down to the mysterious star vehicle.

These things—people—I know not what to call them—must be aquatic; perhaps they live in the canals of the Red Planet. But imagine, Sir—an invisible

mankind! The idea is almost as wonderful and fantastic as something from your novel, "The Time Machine."

Pray give me your comment, and trust in my sanity and accuracy as a reporter!

Yours in friendship,

GREGORY ROLLES.

What he did not tell was the way Nancy had clung to him after, in the warmth of the parlour, and confessed her fear. And he had scorned the idea that these beings could be hostile, and had seen the admiration in her eyes, and had thought that she was, after all, a dashed pretty girl, and perhaps worth braving the wrath of those two very different people for: Edward Rolles, his father, and Bert Neckland, the farm labourer.

At that point Mrs. Grendon came in, and the two young people moved rapidly apart. Mrs. Grendon went more slowly. The new life within her was large now, and she carried herself accordingly. So as not to distress her, they told her nothing of what they had seen. Nor was there time for discussion, for the farmer and his two men came tramping into the kitchen, kicking off their boots and demanding lunch.

It was at lunch a week later, when Gregory was again at the farm, taking with him an article on electricity as a pretext for his visit, that the subject of the stinking dew was first discussed.

Grubby was the first to mention it in Gregory's hearing. Grubby, with Bert Neckland, formed the whole strength of Joseph Grendon's labour force; but whereas Neckland was considered couth enough to board in the farmhouse (he had a gaunt room in the attic), Grubby was fit only to sleep in a little flint-and-chalk hut well away from the farm building. His "house", as he dignified the miserable hut,

stood below the orchard and near the sties, the occupants of which lulled Grubby to sleep with their snorts.

"Reckon we ent ever had a dew like that before, Mr. Grendon," he said, his manner suggesting to Gregory that he had made this observation already this morning; Grubby never ventured to say anything original.

"Heavy as an autumn dew," said the farmer firmly, as if there had been an argument on that point.

Silence fell, broken only by a general munching and, from Grubby, a particular guzzling, as they all made their way through huge platefuls of stewed rabbit and dumplings.

"It weren't no ordinary dew, that I do know," Grubby said after a while.

"It stank of toadstools," Neckland said. "Or rotten pond water."

More munching.

"I have read of freak dews before," Gregory told the company. "And you hear of freak rains, when frogs fall out of the sky. I've even read of hailstones with live frogs and toads embedded in them."

"There's always something beyond belief as you have read of, Master Gregory," Neckland said. "But we happen to be talking about this here dew that fell right on this here farm this here morning. There weren't no frogs in it, either."

"Well it's gone now, so I can't see why you're worried about it," Nancy said.

"We ent ever had a dew like that before, Miss Nancy," Grubby said.

"I know I had to wash my washing again," Mrs. Grendon said. "I left it out all night and it stank really foul this morning."

"It may be something to do with the pond," Gregory said. "Some sort of freak of evaporation."

Neckland snorted. From his position at the top of

the table, the farmer halted his shovelling operations to point a fork at Gregory.

"You may well be right there. Because I tell you what, that there dew only come down on our land and property. A yard the other side of the gate, the road was dry. Bone dry it was."

"Right you are there, master," Neckland agreed. "And while the West Field was dripping with the stuff, I saw for myself that the bracken over the hedge weren't wet at all. Ah, it's a rum go!"

"Say what you like, we ent ever had a dew like it," Grubby said. He appeared to be summing up the feeling of the company.

Leading off the parlour was a smaller room. Although it shared a massive fireplace with the parlour—for the whole house was built round and supported by this central brick stack—fires were rarely lit in the smaller room. This was the Best Room. Here Joseph Grendon occasionally retired to survey—with some severity and discomfort—his accounts. Otherwise the room was scarcely used.

After his meal, Grendon retired belching into the Best Room, and Gregory followed. This was where the farmer kept his modest store of books, his Carlyles, Ainsworths, Ruskins, and Lyttons, together with the copy of "The Time Machine" which Gregory had presented to him at Christmas, complete with a socially-inspired inscription. But the room was chiefly notable for the stuffed animals it contained, some encased in glass.

These animals had evidently been assaulted by a blunder in taxidermy, for they stood in poses that would in life have been beyond them, even supposing them to have been equipped with the extra joints and malformations indicated by their post mortemnal shapes. They numbered among them creatures that bore chance resemblances to owls, dogs, foxes, cats, goats and calves. Only the stuffed fish carried more than a wan likeness to their living

counterparts, and they had felt such an autumn after death that all their scales had been shed like leaves.

Gregory looked doubtfully at these monsters in which man's forming hand was more evident than God's. There were so many of them that some had overflowed into the parlour; in the Best Room, it was their multitude as well as their deformity that appalled. All the same, seeing how gloomily Grendon scowled over his ledger, Gregory said, thinking to cheer the older man, "You should practise some more taxidermy, Joseph."

"Ah." Without looking up.

"The hobby would be pleasant for you."

"Ah." Now he did look up. "You're young and you know only the good side of life. You're ignorant, Master Gregory, for all your university learning. You don't know how the qualities get whittled away from a man until by the time he's my age, there's only persistence left."

"That's not—"

"I shall never do another stuffing job. I ent got time! I ent really got time for nothing but this here old farm."

"But that's not true! You—"

"I say it is true, and I don't talk idle. I pass the time of day with you; I might even say I like you; but you don't *mean* nothing to me." He looked straight at Gregory as he spoke, and then slowly lowered his eyes with what might have been sadness. "Neither does Marjorie mean nothing to me now, though that was different afore we married. I got this here farm, you see, and I'm the farm and it is me."

He was stuck for words, and the beady eyes of the specimens ranged about him stared at him unhelpfully.

"Of course it's hard work," Gregory said.

"You don't understand, bor. Nobody do. This here land is no good. It's barren. Every year, it grows less

and less. It ent got no more life than what these here animals have. So that means I am barren too—year by year, I got less substance."

He stood up suddenly, angry perhaps at himself.

"You better go home, Master Gregory."

"Joe, I'm terribly sorry. I wish I could help . . ."

"I know you mean kindly. You go home while the night's fine." He peered out into the blank yard. "Let's hope we don't get another stinking dewfall tonight."

The strange dew did not fall again. As a topic of conversation, it was limited, and even on the farm, where there was little new to talk about, it was forgotten in a few days. The February passed, being neither much worse nor much better than most Februaries, and ended in heavy rainstorms. March came, letting in a chilly spring over the land. The animals on the farm began to bring forth their young.

They brought them forth in amazing numbers, as if to overturn all the farmer's beliefs in the unproductiveness of his land.

"I never seen anything like it!" Grendon said to Gregory. Nor had Gregory seen the taciturn farmer so excited. He took the young man by the arm and marched him into the barn.

There lay Trix, the nannie goat. Against her flank huddled three little brown and white kids, while a fourth stood nearby, wobbling on its spindly legs.

"Four on 'em! Have you ever heard of a goat throwing off *four* kids? You better write to the papers in London about this, Gregory! But just you come down to the pigsties."

The squealing from the sties was louder than usual. As they marched down the path towards them, Gregory looked up at the great elms, their outlines dusted in green, and thought he detected

something sinister in the noises, something hysterical that was perhaps matched by an element in Grendon's own bearing.

The Grendon pigs were mixed breeds, with a preponderance of Large Blacks. They usually gave litters of something like ten piglets. Now there was not a litter without fourteen in it; one enormous black sow had eighteen small pigs jostling about her. The noise was tremendous and, standing looking down on this swarming life, Gregory told himself that he was foolish to imagine anything uncanny in it; he knew so little about farm life.

"'Course, they ent all going to live," the farmer said. "The old sows ent got enough dugs to feed that brood. But it's a record lot! I reckon you ought to write to that there 'Norwich Advertiser' about it."

Grubby lumbered up with two pails of feed, his great round face flushed as if in rapport with all the fecundity about him.

"Never seen so many pigs," he said. "You ought to write to that there newspaper in Norwich about it, bor. There ent never been so many pigs."

Gregory had no chance to talk to Nancy on the subject. She and her mother had driven to town in the trap, for it was market day in Cottersall. After he had eaten with Grendon and the men—Mrs. Grendon had left them a cold lunch—Gregory went by himself to look about the farm, still with a deep and (he told himself) unreasoning sense of disturbance inside him.

A pale sunshine filled the afternoon. It could not penetrate far down into the water of the pond. But as Gregory stood by the horse trough staring at the expanse of water, he saw that it teemed with young tadpoles and frogs. He went closer. What he had regarded as a sheet of rather stagnant water was alive with small swimming things. As he looked, a great beetle surged out of the depths and seized a tadpole. The tadpoles were also providing food for two ducks

that, with their young, were swimming by the reeds on the far side of the pond. And how many young did the ducks have? An armada of chicks was there, parading in and out of the rushes.

He walked round behind the barn and the cowsheds, where the ground was marshy, and across the bridge at the back of the machine house. The haystacks stood here, and behind them a wild stretch of hedge. As he went, Gregory watched for birds' nests. In the woodpile was a redstart's nest, in the marsh a meadow pipit's, in the hedge nests of sparrows and blackbirds. All were piled high with eggs—far too many eggs.

For a minute, he stood uncertainly, then began to walk slowly back the way he had come. Nancy stood between two of the haystacks. He started in surprise at seeing her. He called her name, but she stood silent with her back to him.

Puzzled, he went forward and touched her on the shoulder. Her head swung round. He saw her long teeth, the yellow curve of bone that had been her nose—but it was a sheep's head, falling backwards off a stick over which her old cloak had been draped. It lay on the ground by her bonnet, and he stared down at it in dismay, trying to quiet the leap of his heart. And at that moment, Neckland jumped out and caught him by the wrist.

"Ha, that gave thee a scare, my hearty, didn't it? I saw 'ee hanging round here. Why don't you get off out of here and never come back, bor? I warned you before, and I ent going to warn you again, do you hear? You leave Nancy alone, you and your books!"

Gregory wrenched his hand away.

"You did this, did you, you bloody ignorant lout? What do you think you are playing at there? How do you think Nancy or her mother would like it if they saw what you had done? Suppose I showed this to Farmer Grendon? Are you off your head, Neckland?"

"Don't you call me a ignorant lout or I'll knock off that there block of yours, that I will. I'm a-giving you a good scare, you cheeky tick, and I'm a-warning you to keep away from here."

"I don't want your warnings, and I refuse to heed them. It's up to the Grendons whether or not I come here, not you. You keep to your place and I'll keep to mine. If you try this sort of thing again, we shall come to blows."

Neckland looked less pugnacious than he had a moment ago. He said, cockily enough, "I ent afraid of you."

"Then I may give you cause to be," Gregory said. Turning on his heel, he walked swiftly away—alert at the same time for an attack from the rear. But Neckland slunk away as silently as he had come.

Crossing the yard, Gregory went over to the stable and saddled Daisy. He swung himself up and rode away without bidding good-bye to anyone.

At one point, he looked over his shoulder. The farm crouched low and dark above the desolate land. Sky predominated over everything. The Earth seemed merely a strip of beach before a great tumbled ocean of air and light and space and things ill-defined; and from that ocean had come . . . he did not know, nor did he know how to find out, except by waiting and seeing if the strange vessel from the seas of space had brought evil or blessing.

Riding into Cottersall, he went straight to the market place. He saw the Grendon trap, with Nancy's little pony, Hetty, between the shafts, standing outside the grocer's shop. Mrs. Grendon and Nancy were just coming out. Jumping to the ground, Gregory led Daisy over to them and bid them good day.

"We are going to call on my friend Mrs. Edwards and her daughters," Mrs. Grendon said.

"I wondered, Mrs. Grendon, if you'd allow me to speak with Nancy privately, just for ten minutes."

Mrs. Grendon was well wrapped against the wind; she made a monumental figure as she looked at her daughter and considered.

"Seeing you talks to her at the farm, I don't see why you shouldn't talk to her here, but I don't want to cause no scandal, Master Gregory, and I'm sure I don't know where you can go to talk private. I mean, folks are more staid in their ways in Norfolk than they used to be in my young days, and I don't want any scandal. Can't it wait till you come to see us at the farm again?"

"If you would be so kind, Mrs. Grendon, I would be very obliged if I might speak privately with her now. My landlady, Mrs. Fenn, has a little downstairs parlour at the back of the shop, and I know she would let us speak there. It would be quite respectable."

"Drat respectable! Let people think what they will, I say." All the same, she stood for some time in meditation. Nancy remained by her mother with her eyes on the ground. Gregory looked at her and seemed to see her anew. Under her blue coat, fur-trimmed, she wore her orange-and-brown squared gingham dress: she had a bonnet on her head. Her complexion was pure and blemishless, her skin as firm and delicate as a plum, and her dark eyes were hidden under long lashes. Her lips were steady, pale, and clearly defined, with appealing tucks at each corner. He felt almost like a thief, stealing a sight of her beauty while she was not regarding him.

"I'm going on to Mrs. Edwards," Marjorie Grendon declared at last. "I don't care what you two do so long as you behave—but I shall, mind, if you aren't with me in a half-hour, Nancy, do you hear?"

"Yes, mother."

The baker's shop was in the next street. Gregory and Nancy walked there in silence. Gregory shut Daisy in the stable and they went together into the parlour through the back door. At this time of day,

Mr. Fenn was resting upstairs and his wife looking after the shop, so the little room was empty.

Nancy sat upright in a chair and said, "Well, Gregory, what's all this about? Fancy dragging me off from my mother like that in the middle of town!"

"Nancy, don't be cross. I had to see you."

She pouted. "You come out to the old farm often enough and don't show any particular wish to see me there."

"That's nonsense. I always come to see you—lately in particular. Besides, you're more interested in Bert Neckland, aren't you?"

"Bert Neckland, indeed! Why should I be interested in him? Not that it's any of your business if I am."

"It is my business, Nancy. I love you, Nancy!"

He had not meant to blurt it out in quite that fashion, but now it was out, it was out, and he pressed home his disadvantage by crossing the room, kneeling at her feet, and taking her hands in his.

"I thought you only came out to the farm to see my father."

"It was like that at first, Nancy, but no more."

"You've got interested in farming now, haven't you? That's what you come for now, isn't it?"

"Well, I certainly am interested in the farm, but I want to talk about you. Nancy, darling Nancy, say that you like me just a little. Encourage me somewhat."

"You are a very fine gentleman, Gregory, and I feel very kind towards you, to be sure, but . . ."

"But?"

She gave him the benefit of her downcast eyes again.

"Your station in life is very different from mine, and besides—well, you don't *do* anything."

He was shocked into silence. With the natural egotism of youth, he had not seriously thought that she could have any firm objection to him; but in her

words he suddenly saw the truth of his position, at least as it was revealed to her.

"Nancy—I—well, it's true I do not seem to you to be working at present. But I do a lot of reading and studying here, and I write to several important people in the world. And all the time I am coming to a great decision about what my career will be. I do assure you I am no loafer, if that's what you think."

"No, I don't think that. But Bert says you often spend a convivial evening in that there 'Wayfarer'."

"Oh, he does, does he? And what business is it of his if I do—or of yours, come to that? What a damned cheek!"

She stood up. "If you have nothing left to say but a lot of swearing, I'll be off to join my mother, if you don't mind."

"Oh, by Jove, I'm making a mess of this!" He caught her wrist. "Listen, my sweet thing. I ask you only this, that you try and look on me favourably. And also that you let me say a word about the farm. Some strange things are happening there, and I seriously don't like to think of you being there at night. All these young things being born, all these little pigs—it's uncanny!"

"I don't see what's uncanny no more than my father does. I know how hard he works, and he's done a good job rearing his animals, that's all. He's the best farmer round Cottersall by a long chalk."

"Oh, certainly. He's a wonderful man. But he didn't put seven or eight eggs into a hedge-sparrow's nest, did he? He didn't fill the pond with tadpoles and newts till it looks like a broth, did he? Something strange is happening on your farm this year, Nancy, and I want to protect you if I can."

The earnestness with which he spoke, coupled perhaps with his proximity and the ardent way he pressed her hand, went a good way toward mollifying Nancy.

"Dear Gregory, you don't know anything about

farm life, I don't reckon, for all your books. But you're very sweet to be concerned."

"I shall always be concerned about you, Nancy, you beautiful creature."

"You'll make me blush!"

"Please do, for then you look even lovelier than usual!" He put an arm round her. When she looked up at him, he caught her up close to his chest and kissed her fervently.

She gasped and broke away, but not with too great haste.

"Oh, Gregory! Oh, Gregory! I must go to mother now!"

"Another kiss first! I can't let you go until I get another."

He took it, and stood by the door trembling with excitement as she left. "Come and see us again soon," she whispered.

"With dearest pleasure," he said. But the next visit held more dread than pleasure.

The big cart was standing in the yard full of squealing piglets when Gregory arrived. The farmer and Neckland were bustling about it. The farmer, shrugging into his overcoat, greeted Gregory cheerfully.

"I've a chance to make a good quick profit on these little chaps. Old sows can't feed them, but sucking pigs fetches its price in Norwich, so Bert and me are going to drive over to Heigham and put them on the train."

"They're grown since I last saw them!"

"Ah, they put on over two pounds a day. Bert, we'd better get a net and spread over this lot, or they'll be diving out. They're that lively!"

The two men made their way over to the barn, clomping through the mud. Mud squelched behind Gregory. He turned.

In the muck between the stables and the cart, footprints appeared, two parallel tracks. They seemed to imprint themselves with no agency but their own. A cold flow of acute supernatural terror overcame Gregory, so that he could not move. The scene seemed to go grey and palsied as he watched the tracks come towards him.

The carthorse neighed uneasily, the prints reached the cart, the cart creaked, as if something had climbed aboard. The piglets squealed with terror. One dived clear over the wooden sides. Then a terrible silence fell.

Gregory still could not move. Hie heard an unaccountable sucking noise in the cart, but his eyes remained rooted on the muddy tracks. Those impressions were of something other than a man: something with dragging feet that were in outline something like a seal's flippers. Suddenly he found his voice, "Mr. Grendon!" he cried.

Only as the farmer and Bert came running from the barn with the net did Gregory dare look into the cart.

One last piglet, even as he looked, seemed to be deflating rapidly, like a rubber balloon collapsing. It went limp and lay silent among the other little empty bags of pig skin. The cart creaked. Something splashed heavily off across the farm-yard in the direction of the pond.

Grendon did not see. He had run to the cart and was staring like Gregory in dismay at the deflated corpses. Neckland stared too, and was the first to find his voice.

"Some sort of disease got 'em all, just like that! Must be one of them there new diseases from the continent of Europe!"

"It's no disease," Gregory said. He could hardly speak, for his mind had just registered the fact that there were no bones left in or amid the deflated pig

bodies. "It's no disease—look, the pig that got away is still alive."

He pointed to the animal that had jumped from the cart. It had injured its leg in the process, and now lay in the ditch some feet away, panting. The farmer went over to it and lifted it out.

"It escaped the disease by jumping out," Neckland said. "Master, we better go and see how the rest of them is down in the sties."

"Ah, that we had," Grendon said. He handed the pig over to Gregory, his face set. "No good taking one alone to market. I'll get Grubby to unharness the horse. Meanwhile, perhaps you'd be good enough to take this little chap in to Marjorie. At least we can all eat a bit of roast pig for dinner tomorrow."

"Mr. Grendon, this is no disease. Have the veterinarian over from Heigham and let him examine these bodies."

"Don't you tell me how to run my farm, young man. I've got trouble enough."

Despite this rebuff, Gregory could not keep away. He had to see Nancy, and he had to see what occurred at the farm. The morning after the horrible thing happened to the pigs, he received a letter from his most admired correspondent, Mr. H. G. Wells, one paragraph of which read: "At bottom, I think I am neither optimist nor pessimist. I tend to believe both that we stand on the threshold of an epoch of magnificent progress—certainly such an epoch is within our grasp—and that we may have reached the *"fin du globe"* prophesied by our gloomier *fin de siècle* prophets. I am not at all surprised to hear that such a vast issue may be resolving itself on a remote farm near Cottersall, Norfolk—all unknown to anyone but the two of us. Do not think that I am in other than a state of terror, even when I cannot help exclaiming 'What a lark!' "

Too preoccupied to be as excited over such a letter

as he would ordinarily have been, Gregory tucked it away in his jacket pocket and went to saddle up Daisy.

Before lunch, he stole a kiss from Nancy, and planted another on her over-heated left cheek as she stood by the vast range in the kitchen. Apart from that, there was little pleasure in the day. Grendon was reassured to find that none of the other piglets had fallen ill of the strange shrinking disease, but he remained alert against the possibility of it striking again. Meanwhile, another miracle had occurred. In the lower pasture, in a tumble-down shed, he had a cow that had given birth to four calves during the night. He did not expect the animal to live, but the calves were well enough, and being fed from a bottle by Nancy.

The farmer's face was dull, for he had been up all night with the labouring cow, and he sat down thankfully at the head of the table as the roast pig arrived on its platter.

It proved uneatable. In no time, they were all flinging down implements in disgust. The flesh had a bitter taste for which Neckland was the first to account.

"It's diseased!" he growled. "This here animal had the disease all the time. We didn't ought to eat this here meat or we may all be dead ourselves inside of a week."

They were forced to make a snack on cold salted beef and cheese and pickled onions, none of which Mrs. Grendon could face in her condition. She retreated upstairs in tears at the thought of the failure of her carefully prepared dish, and Nancy ran after her to comfort her.

After the dismal meal, Gregory spoke to Grendon.

"I have decided I must go to Norwich tomorrow for a few days, Mr. Grendon," he said. "You are in trouble here, I believe. Is there anything, any busi-

ness, I can transact for you in the city? Can I find you a veterinary surgeon there?"

Grendon clapped his shoulder. "I know you mean well, and I thank 'ee for it, but you don't seem to realize that veterinaries cost a load of money and aren't always too helpful when they do come. Just suppose we had some young idiot here who told us all our stock is poisoned and we had to kill it? That would be a right look-out, eh?"

"Just because Gregory Rolles has plenty of money, he thinks everyone has," Neckland sneered.

The farmer turned furiously on him. "Who asked you to open your trap, bor? You keep your trap shut when there's a private conversation going on as don't concern you at all. Why aren't you out cleaning down the cowshed, since you ett all that last loaf?"

When Neckland had gone, Grendon said, "Bert's a good lad, but he don't like you at all. Now you was saying we had trouble here. But a farm is always trouble, Gregory—some years one sort of trouble, some years another. But I ent ever seen such fine growth as this year, and I tell 'ee straight I'm delighted, proper delighted. Some pigs have died, but that ent going to stop me doing my best by all the rest of 'em."

"But they will be unmarketable if they all taste like the one today."

Grendon smote his palm. "You're a real worrier. They may grow out of this bitter taste. And then again, if they don't, people have to buy them before they can taste them, don't they? I'm a poor man, Gregory, and when a bit of fortune comes my way, I can't afford to let it get away. In fact, I tell 'ee this, and even Bert don't know it yet, but tomorrow or the next day, I got Seeley the builder coming over here to put me up some more wood sheds down by Grubby's hut, to give the young animals more room."

"Good. Then let me do something for you, Joseph, in return for all your kindness to me. Let me bring a

vet back from Norwich at my own expense, just to have a look round, nothing more."

"Blow me if you aren't stubborn as they come. I'm telling you, same as my dad used to say, if I finds any person on my land as I didn't ask here, I'm getting that there gun of mine down and I'm peppering him with buckshot, same as I did with them two old tramps last year. Fair enough, bor?"

"I suppose so."

"Then I must go and see to the cow. And stop worrying about what you don't understand."

After the farmer had gone, Gregory stood for a long time looking out of the window, waiting for Nancy to come down, worrying over the train of events. But the view was peaceful enough. He was the only person worrying, he reflected. Even the shrewd Mr. H. G. Wells, his correspondent, seemed to take his reports with a pinch of salt—he who of all men in England should sympathetically receive the news of the miraculous when it came to Earth, even if it failed to arrive in the form predicted in his recent novel, "The Wonderful Visit". Be that as it might, he was going to Norwich and the wise uncle who lived there as soon as he could—as soon, in fact, as he had kissed dear Nancy good-bye.

The wise uncle was indeed sympathetic. He was altogether a gentler man than his brother Edward, Gregory's father. He looked with sympathy at the plan of the farm that Gregory drew, he looked with sympathy at the sketch of the muddy footprint, he listened with sympathy to an account of what happened. And at the end of it all he said, "Ghosts!"

When Gregory tried to argue with him, he said firmly, "My dear boy, I fear the modern marvels of our age have gone to your head. You know of such engineering structures as the cantilever bridge over the Firth of Forth, and you know as we all do of the colossal tower Eiffel has built in Paris—though if it stands ten years, I'll eat my hat. Now, no one will

deny these things are marvellous, but they are things that rest on the ground. You're trying to tell me that engineers on this world or some other world might build a machine—a vehicle—that could fly from one heavenly body to another. Well then, *I'm* telling you that no engineer can do such a thing—and I'm not just saying that, but I'm quoting a law about it. There's a law about engineers not being able to sail in some sort of damned Eiffel Tower with engines from Mars to Earth, or the Sun to Earth, or whatever you will—a law to be read in your Bible and echoed in the pages of 'The Cornhill'. No, my boy, the modern age has gone to your head, but it's old-fashioned ghosts that have gone to your farm."

So Gregory walked into the city, and inspected the booksellers, and made several purchases, and never doubted for a moment that his uncle, though infinitely sympathetic, and adroit at slipping one a sovereign on parting, was sadly less wise than he had hitherto seemed: a discovery that seemed to reflect how Gregory had grown up and how times were changing.

But Norwich was a pleasant city and his uncle's house a comfortable house in which to stay, and he lingered there a week where he had meant to spend only three days at the most.

Consequently, conscience stirred in him when he again approached the Grendon farm along the rough road from Cottersall. He was surprised to see how the countryside had altered since he was last this way. New foliage gleamed everywhere, and even the heath looked a happier place. But as he came to the farm, he saw how overgrown it was. Great ragged elder and towering cow parsley had shot up, so that at first they hid all the buildings. He fancied the farm had been spirited away until, spurring Daisy on, he saw the black mill emerge from behind a clump of nearby growth. The south meadows were deep in rank grass. Even the elms seemed much shaggier

than before and loomed threateningly over the house.

As he clattered over the flat wooden bridge and through the open gate into the yard, Gregory noted huge hairy nettles craning out of the adjoining ditches. Birds fluttered everywhere. Yet the impression he received was one of death rather than life. A great quiet lay over the place, as if it were under a curse that eliminated noise and hope.

He realized this effect was partly because Lardie, the young bitch collie who had taken the place of Cuff, was not running up barking as she generally did with visitors. The yard was deserted. Even the customary fowls had gone. As he led Daisy into the stables, he saw a heavy piebald in the first stall and recognized it as Dr. Crouchorn's. His anxieties took more definite shape.

Since the stable was now full, he led his mare across to the stone trough by the pond and hitched her there before walking over to the house. The front door was open. Great ragged dandelions grew against the porch. The creeper, hitherto somewhat sparse, pressed into the lower windows. A movement in the rank grass caught his eye and he looked down, drawing back his riding boot. An enormous toad crouched under weed, the head of a still writhing grass snake in his mouth. The toad seemed to eye Gregory fixedly, as if trying to determine whether the man envied it its gluttony. Shuddering in disgust, he hurried into the house.

Three of Trix's kids, well grown now, stutted about the parlour, nibbling at the carpet and climbing into the massive armchairs, staring at a stuffed caricature of a goat that stood in its glass case by the window. Judging by the chaos in the room, they had been there some while, and had had a game on the table. But they possessed the room alone, and a quick glance into the kitchen revealed nobody there either.

Muffled sounds came from upstairs. The stairs curled round the massive chimneypiece, and were shut from the lower rooms by a latched door. Gregory had never been invited upstairs, but he did not hesitate. Throwing the door open, he started up the dark stairwell, and almost at once ran into a body.

Its softness told him that this was Nancy; she stood in the dark weeping. Even as he caught her and breathed her name, she broke from his grasp and ran from him up the stairs. He could hear the noises more clearly now, and the sound of crying—though at the moment he was not listening. Nancy ran to a door on the landing nearest to the top of the stairs, burst into the room beyond, and closed it. When Gregory tried the latch, he heard the bolt slide to on the other side.

"Nancy!" he called. "Don't hide from me! What is it? What's happening?"

She made no answer. As he stood there baffled against the door, the next door along the passage opened and Doctor Crouchorn emerged, clutching his little black bag. He was a tall, sombre man, with deep lines on his face that inspired such fear into his patients that a remarkable percentage of them did as he bid and recovered. Even here, he wore the top hat that, simply by remaining constantly in position, contributed to the doctor's fame in the neighbourhood.

"What's the trouble, Doctor Crouchorn?" Gregory asked, as the medical man shut the door behind him and started down the stairs. "Has the plague struck this house, or something equally terrible?"

"Plague, young man, plague? No, it is something much more unnatural than that."

He stared at Gregory unsmilingly, as if promising himself inwardly not to move a muscle again until Gregory asked the obvious.

"What did you call for, doctor?"

"The hour of Mrs. Grendon's confinement struck during the night," he said, still poised on the top step.

A wave of relief swept over Gregory. He had forgotten Nancy's mother! "She's had her baby? Was it a boy?"

The doctor nodded in slow motion. "She bore two boys, young man." He hesitated, and then a muscle in his face twitched and he said in a rush, "She also bore seven daughters. Nine children! And they all—they all live. It's impossible. Until I die—"

He could not finish. Tipping his hat, he hurried down the stairs, leaving Gregory to look fixedly at the wallpaper while his mind whirled as if it would convert itself into liquid. Nine children! Nine! It was as if she were no different from an animal in a sty. And the wallpaper pattern took on a diseased and vivid look as if the house itself embodied sickness. The mewling cries from the bedroom seemed also the emblem of something inhuman calling its need.

He stood there in a daze, the sickly infant cries boring into him. From beyond the stone walls that oppressed him, he heard the noise of a horse ridden at hard gallop over the wooden bridge and down the track to Cottersall, dying with distance. From Nancy's room came no sound. Gregory guessed she had hidden herself from him for shame, and at last stirred himself into moving down the dark and curving stairwell. A stable cat scuttled out from under the bottom stair, a dozen baby tabbies in pursuit. The goats still held possession of the room. The fire was but scattered ashes in the hearth, and had not been tended since the crisis of the night.

"I bet you're surprised!"

Gregory swung round. From the kitchen came Grubby, clutching a wedge of bread and meat in his fist. He chewed with his mouth open, grinning at Gregory.

"Farmer Grendon be a proper ram!" he exclaimed. "Ent no other man in this county could beget himself nine kids at one go!"

"Where is the farmer?"

"I say there ent no other man in this here county—"

"Yes, I heard what you said. Where is the farmer?"

"Working, I suppose. But I tell 'ee, bor, there ent no other man—"

Leaving Grubby munching and talking, Gregory strode out into the yard. He came on Grendon round the corner of the house. The farmer had a pitchfork full of hay, which he was carrying over his shoulder into the cowsheds. Gregory stood in his way but he pushed past.

"I want to speak to you, Joseph."

"There's work to be done. Pity you can't see that."

"I want to speak about your wife."

Grendon made no reply. He worked like a demon, tossing the hay down, turning for more. In any case, it was difficult to talk. The cows and calves, closely confined, seemed to set up a perpetual uneasy noise of lowing and un-cow-like grunts. Gregory followed the farmer round to the hayrick, but the man walked like one possessed. His eyes seemed sunk into his head, his mouth was puckered until his lips were invisible. When Gregory laid a hand on his arm, he shook it off. Stabbing up another great load of hay, he swung back towards the sheds so violently that Gregory had to jump out of his way.

Gregory lost his temper. Following Grendon back into the cowshed, he swung the bottom of the two-part door shut, and bolted it on the outside. When Grendon came back, he did not budge.

"Joseph, what's got into you? Why are you suddenly so heartless? Surely your wife needs you by her?"

His eyes had a curious blind look as he turned them at Gregory. He held the pitchfork before him

in both hands almost like a weapon as he said, "I been with her all night, bor, while she brought forth her increase."

"But now—"

"She got a nursing woman from Dereham Cottages with her now. I been with her all night. Now I got to see to the farm—things keep growing, you know."

"They're growing too much, Joseph. Stop and think—"

"I've no time for talking." Dropping the pitchfork, he elbowed Gregory out of the way, unbolted the door, and flung it open. Grasping Gregory firmly by the biceps of one arm, he began to propel him along to the vegetable beds down by South Meadows.

The early lettuce were gigantic here. Everything bristled out of the ground. Recklessly, Grendon ran among the lines of new green, pulling up fists full of young radish, carrots, spring onions, scattering them over his shoulder as fast as he plucked them from the ground.

"See, Gregory—all bigger than you ever seen 'em, and weeks early! The harvest is going to be a bumper. Look at the fields! Look at the orchard!" With wide gesture, he swept a hand towards the lines of trees, buried in the mounds of snow-and-pink of their blossom. "Whatever happens, we got to take advantage of it. It may not happen another year. Why—it's like a fairy story!"

He said no more. Turning, he seemed already to have forgotten Gregory. Eyes down at the ground that had suddenly achieved such abundance, he marched back towards the sheds, from whence now came the sound of Neckland washing out milk churns.

The spring sun was warm on Gregory's back. He told himself that everything looked normal. The farm was flourishing. From beyond the sties came

shouts, distantly, and the sounds of men working, where the builder was preparing to erect more sheds. Perhaps, he told himself dully, he was worrying about nothing. Slowly, he walked towards the back of the house. There was nothing he could do here; it was time to return to Cottersall; but first he must see Nancy.

Nancy was in the kitchen. Neckland had brought her in a stoup of fresh milk, and she was supping it wearily from a ladle.

"Oh, Greg, I'm sorry I ran from you. I was so upset." She came to him, still holding the ladle but dangling her arms over his shoulders in a familiar way she had not used before. "Poor mother, I fear her mind is unhinged with—with bearing so many children. She's talking such strange stuff as I never heard before, and I do believe she fancies as she's a child again."

"Is it to be wondered at?" he said, smoothing her hair with his hand. "She'll be better once she's recovered from the shock."

They kissed each other, and after a minute she passed him a ladleful of milk. He drank and then spat it out in disgust.

"Ugh! What's got into the milk? Is Neckland trying to poison you or something? Have you tasted it? It's as bitter as sloes!"

She pulled a puzzled face. "I thought it tasted rather strange, but not unpleasant. Here, let me try again."

"No, it's too horrible. Some Sloan's Liniment must have got mixed in it."

Despite his warning, she put her lips to the metal spoon and sipped, then shook her head. "You're imagining things, Greg. It does taste a bit different, 'tis true, but there's nothing wrong with it."

"Sweetheart, it's horrible. I'm going to get your father to taste it, and see what he thinks."

"I wouldn't bother him just now, Greg, if I was you. You know how busy he is, and tired, and attending on mother during the night has put him back in his work. I will mention it to him at dinner—which I must now prepare. Them there goats have made such a muck in here, not to mention that Grubby! You'll stay to take a bite with us, I hope?"

"No, Nancy, I'm off now. I have a letter awaiting me that I must answer; it arrived when I was in Norwich."

She bit her lip and snapped her fingers. "There, how terrible awful you'll think me! I never asked you how you enjoyed yourself in the big city! It must be wonderful to be a man of leisure, never with no work to do nor meals to prepare."

"You still hold that against me! Listen, my lovely Nancy, this letter is from a Dr. Hudson-Ward, an old acquaintance of my father's. He is headmaster of a school in Gloucester, and he wishes me to join the staff there as teacher on most favourable terms. So you see I may not be idle much longer!"

Laughing, she clung to him. "That's wonderful, my darling! What a handsome schoolmaster you will make. But Gloucester—that's over the other side of the country. I suppose we shan't be seeing you again once you get there."

"Nothing's settled yet, Nancy."

"You'll be gone in a week and we shan't never see you again. Once you get to that old school, you will never think of your Nancy no more."

He cupped her face in his hands. "Are you my Nancy? Do you care for me?"

Her eyelashes came over her dark eyes. "Greg, things are so muddled here—I mean—yes, I do care, I dread to think I'd not see you again."

Recalling her saying that, he rode away a quarter of an hour later very content at heart—and entirely

neglectful of the dangers to which he left her exposed.

Rain fell lightly as Gregory Rolles made his way that evening to the "Wayfarer" inn. His friend Bruce Fox was already there, ensconced in one of the snug seats by the ingle nook.

On this occasion, Fox was more interested in purveying details of his sister's forthcoming wedding than in listening to what Gregory had to tell, and since some of his future brother-in-law's friends soon arrived, and had to buy and be bought libation, the evening became a merry and thoughtless one. And in a short while, the ale having its good effect, Gregory also forgot what he wanted to say and began wholeheartedly to enjoy the company.

Next morning, he awoke with a heavy head and in a dismal state of mind. Mrs. Fenn, clattering round the room lighting his fire, did not improve matters; he could tell from her demeanour that he had come home late and made a noise on the stairs. But the Mrs. Fenns of this world, he reflected irritably, were born to suffer such indignities, and the more regularly the better. He told himself this thought was not in accord with his socialist principles, but they felt as sluggish as his liver this morning.

The day was too wet for him to go out and take exercise. He sat moodily in a chair by the window, delaying an answer to Dr. Hudson-Ward, the headmaster. Lethargically, he turned to a small leather-bound volume on serpents that he had acquired in Norwich a few days earlier. After a while, a passage caught his particular attention:

"Most serpents of the venomous variety, with the exception of the opisthoglyphs, release their victims from their fangs after striking. The victims die in some cases in but a few seconds, while in other cases the onset of moribundity may be delayed by hours or days. The saliva of some serpents contains not only

venom but a special digestive virtue. The deadly Coral Snake of Brazil, though attaining no more than a foot in length, has this virtue in abundance. Accordingly, when it bites an animal or a human being, the victim not only dies in profound agony in a matter of seconds, but his interior parts are then dissolved, so that even the bones become no more than jelly. Then may the little serpent suck all of the victim out as a kind of soup or broth from the original wound in its skin, which latter alone remains intact."

For a long while, Gregory sat where he was in the window, with the book open in his lap, thinking about the Grendon farm, and about Nancy. He reproached himself for having done so little for his friends there, and gradually resolved on a plan of action the next time he rode out; but his visit was to be delayed for some days: the wet weather had set in with more determination than the end of April and the beginning of May generally allowed.

Despite that, he heard news of Grendon on the second day of rain as he took his supper with the Fenns downstairs. That was market day, and then the baker's wife said, "That there idiot labourer on Joe Grendon's place is going to get himself locked up if he ent careful. Did you hear about him today, Master Gregory?"

"What did he do, Mrs. Fenn?"

"Why, what didn't he do? Delivered the milk round as usual, so I hear, and nobody wouldn't buy none, seeing as it has been off for the past I-don't-know-how-long. So Grubby swore terrible and vowed he had the best milk in town, and took a great sup at the churn to prove it. And then them two Betts boys started throwing stones, and of course that set Grubby off! He caught one of 'em and ducked his head in the milk, and then flung the bucket right smack through his father's nice glass window. Imagine that! So out come old man Betts and his great big

missus, and they lambasts old Grubby with beansticks till he drives off cursing and vowing he'll never sell nobody good milk no more!"

The baker laughed. "That would have been a sight worth seeing of! I reckon they all gone mad out at Joe's place. Old Seeley the builder come in yesterday morning, and he reckon Joe's doing better this year than what he ever did, while everyone else round here is having a thin time. According to Seeley, Marjorie Grendon had quins, but you know old Seeley is a bit of a joker. Dr. Crouchorn would have let on if she'd had quins, I reckon."

"Doctor Crouchorn was weeping drunk last night, from all accounts."

"So I hear. That ent like him, be it?"

"First time it was ever known, though they do say he liked his bottle when he was a youngster."

Listening to the gossip as it shuttled back and forth between husband and wife, Gregory found little appetite for his stew. Moodily, he returned to his room and tried to concentrate on a letter to the worthy Dr. Hudson-Ward in the county of Gloucestershire. He knew he should take the job, indeed he felt inclined to do so; but first he knew he had to see Nancy safe. The indecision he felt caused him to delay answering the doctor until the next day, when he feebly wrote that he would be glad to accept the post offered at the price offered, but begged to have a week to think about it. When he took the letter down to the post woman in "The Three Poachers", the rain was still falling.

One morning, the rains were suddenly vanished, the blue and wide East Anglian skies were back, and Gregory saddled up Daisy and rode out along the miry track he had so often taken. As he arrived at the farm, Grubby and Neckland were at work in the ditch, unblocking it with shovels. He saluted them

and rode in. As he was about to put the mare into the stables, he saw Grendon and Nancy standing on the patch of waste ground under the windowless east side of the house. He went slowly to join them, noting as he walked how dry the ground was here, as if no rain had fallen in a fortnight. But this observation was drowned in shock as he saw the nine little crosses Grendon was sticking into nine freshly-turned mounds of earth.

Nancy stood weeping. They both looked up as Gregory approached, but Grendon went stubbornly on with his task.

"Oh, Nancy, Joseph, I'm so sorry about this!" Gregory exclaimed. "To think that they've all—but where's the parson? Where's the parson, Joseph? Why are *you* burying them, without a proper service or anything?"

"I told father, but he took no heed!" Nancy exclaimed.

Grendon had reached the last grave. He seized the last crude wooden cross, lifted it above his head and stabbed it down into the ground as if he would pierce the heart of what lay under it. Only then did he straighten and speak.

"We don't need a parson here. I've no time to waste with parsons. I have work to do if you ent."

"But these are your children, Joseph! What has got into you?"

"They are part of the farm now, as they always was." He turned, rolling his shirt sleeves further up his brawny arms, and strode off in the direction of the ditching activities.

Gregory took Nancy in his arms and looked at her tear-stained face. "What a time you must have been having these last few days!"

"I—I thought you'd gone to Gloucester, Greg! Why didn't you come? Every day I waited for you to come!"

"It was so wet and flooded."

"It's been lovely weather since you were last here. Look how everything has grown!"

"It poured with rain every single day in Cottersall."

"Well, I never! That explains why there is so much water flowing in the Oast and in the ditches. But we've had only a few light showers."

"Nancy, tell me, how did these poor little mites die?"

"I'd rather not say, if you don't mind."

"Why didn't your father get in Parson Landson? How could he be so lacking in feeling?"

"Because he didn't want anyone from the outside world to know. That's why he's sent the builders away again. You see—oh, I must tell you, my dear—it's mother. She has gone completely off her head, completely! It was the evening before last, when she took her first turn outside the back door."

"You don't mean to say she—"

"Ow, Greg, you're hurting my arms! She—she crept upstairs when we weren't noticing and she—she stifled each of the babies in turn, Greg, under the best goose-feather pillow."

He could feel the colour leaving his cheeks. Solicitously, she led him to the back of the house. They sat together on the orchard railings while he digested the words in silence.

"How is your mother now, Nancy?"

"She's silent. Father had to bar her in her room for safety. Last night she screamed a lot. But this morning she's quiet."

He looked dazedly about him. The appearance of everything was speckled, as if the return of his blood to his head had somehow infected it with a rash. The blossom had gone almost entirely from the fruit trees in the orchard and already the embryo apples showed signs of swelling. Nearby, broad beans bowed under enormous pods. Seeing his glance,

Nancy dipped into her apron pocket and produced a bunch of shining crimson radishes as big as tangerines.

"Have one of these. They're crisp and wet and hot, just as they should be."

Indifferently, he accepted and bit the tempting globe. At once he had to spit the portion out. There again was that vile bitter flavour!

"Oh, but they're lovely!" Nancy protested.

"Not even 'rather strange' now—simply 'lovely'? Nancy, don't you see, something uncanny and awful is taking place here. I'm sorry, but I can't see otherwise. You and your father should leave here at once."

"*Leave* here, Greg? Just because you don't like the taste of these lovely radishes? How can we leave here? Where should we go? See this here house? My granddad died here, and his father before him. It's our *place.* We can't just up and off, not even after this bit of trouble. Try another radish."

"For heaven's sake, Nancy, they taste as if the flavour was intended for creatures with a palate completely different from ours . . . Oh . . ." He stared at her. "And perhaps they are. Nancy, I tell you—"

He broke off, sliding from the railing. Neckland had come up from one side, still plastered in mud from his work in the ditch, his collarless shirt flapping open. In his hand, he grasped an ancient and military-looking pistol.

"I'll fire this if you come nearer," he said. "It goes okey, never worry, and it's loaded, Master Gregory. Now you're a-going to listen to me!"

"Bert, put that thing away!" Nancy exclaimed. She moved forward to him, but Gregory pulled her back and stood before her.

"Don't be a bloody idiot, Neckland. Put it away!"

"I'll shoot you, bor, I'll shoot you, I swear, if you mucks about." His eyes were glaring, and the look on

his dark face left no doubt that he meant what he said. "You're going to swear to me that you're going to clear off of this farm on that nag of yours and never come back again."

"I'm going straight to tell my father, Bert," Nancy warned.

The pistol twitched.

"If you move, Nancy, I warn you I'll shoot this fine chap of yours in the leg. Besides, your father don't care about Master Gregory any more—he's got better things to worry him."

"Like finding out what's happening here?" Gregory said. "Listen, Neckland, we're all in trouble. This farm is being run by a group of nasty little monsters. You can't see them because they're invisible—"

The gun exploded. As he spoke, Nancy had attempted to run off. Without hesitating, Neckland fired down at Gregory's knees. Gregory felt the shot pluck his trouser leg and knew himself unharmed. With the knowledge came rage. He flung himself at Neckland and hit him hard over the heart. Falling back, Neckland dropped the pistol and swung his fist wildly. Gregory struck him again. As he did so, the other grabbed him and they began furiously hitting each other. When Gregory broke free, Neckland grappled with him again. There was more pummelling of ribs.

"Let me go, you swine!" Gregory shouted. He hooked his foot behind Neckland's ankle, and they both rolled over onto the grass. At this point, a sort of flood bank had been raised long ago between the house and the low-lying orchard. Down this the two men rolled, fetching up sharply against the stone wall of the kitchen. Neckland got the worst of it, catching his head on the corner, and lay there stunned. Gregory found himself looking at two feet encased in ludicrous stockings. Slowly, he rose to his feet, and confronted Mrs. Grendon at less than a yard's distance. She was smiling.

He stood there, and gradually straightened his back, looking at her anxiously.

"So there you are, Jackie, my Jackalums," she said. The smile was wider now and less like a smile. "I wanted to talk to you. You are the one who knows about the things that walk on the lines, aren't you?"

"I don't understand, Mrs. Grendon."

"Don't call me that there daft old name, sonnie. You know all about the little grey things that aren't supposed to be there, don't you?"

"Oh, those . . . Suppose I said I did know?"

"The other naughty children will pretend they don't know what I mean, but you know, don't you? You know about the little grey things."

The sweat stood out on his brow. She had moved nearer. She stood close, staring into his eyes, not touching him; but he was acutely conscious that she could touch him at any moment. From the corner of his eye, he saw Neckland stir and crawl away from the house, but there were other things to occupy him.

"These little grey things," he said. "Did you save the nine babies from them?"

"They grey things wanted to kiss them, you see, but I couldn't let them. I was clever. I hid them under the goose-feather pillow and now even *I* can't find them!" She began to laugh, making a horrible low whirring sound in her throat.

"They're small and grey and wet, aren't they?" Gregory said sharply. "They've got big feet, webbed like frogs, but they're heavy and short, aren't they, and they have fangs like a snake, haven't they?"

She looked doubtful. Then her eye seemed to catch a movement. She looked fixedly to one side. "Here come one now, the female one," she said.

Gregory turned to look where she did. Nothing was visible. His mouth was dry. "How many are there, Mrs. Grendon?"

Then he saw the short grass stir, flatten, and raise near at hand, and let out a cry of alarm. Wrenching

off his riding boot, he swung it in an arc, low above the ground. It struck something concealed in thin air. Almost at once, he received a terrific kick in the thigh, and fell backwards. Despite the hurt, fear made him jump up almost at once.

Mrs. Grendon was changing. Her mouth collapsed as if it would run off one corner of her face. Her head sagged to one side. Her shoulders fell. A deep crimson blush momentarily suffused her features, then drained, and as it drained she dwindled like a deflated rubber balloon. Gregory sank to his knees, whimpering, buried his face in his hands and pressed his hands to the grass. Darkness overcame him.

His senses must have left him only for a moment. When he pulled himself up again, the almost empty bag of woman's clothes was still settling slowly on the ground.

"Joseph! Joseph!" he yelled. Nancy had fled. In a distracted mixture of panic and fury, he dragged his boot on again and rushed round the house towards the cowsheds.

Neckland stood half-way between barn and mill, rubbing his skull. In his rattled state, the sight of Gregory apparently in full pursuit made him run away.

"Neckland!" Gregory shouted. He ran like mad for the other. Neckland bolted for the mill, jumped inside, tried to pull the door to, lost his nerve, and ran up the wooden stairs. Gregory bellowed after him.

The pursuit took them right up to the top of the mill. Neckland had lost too much wit even to kick over the bolt of the trapdoor. Gregory burst it up and climbed out panting. Thoroughly cowed, Neckland backed towards the opening until he was almost out on the little platform above the sails.

"You'll fall out, you idiot," Gregory warned. "Listen, Neckland, you have no reason to fear me. I want

no enmity between us. There's a bigger enemy we must fight. Look!"

He came towards the low door and looked down at the dark surface of the pond. Neckland grabbed the overhead pulley for security and said nothing.

"Look down at the pond," Gregory said. "That's where the Aurigans live. My God—Bert, look, there one goes!"

The urgency in his voice made the farm hand look down where he pointed. Together, the two men watched as a depression slid over the black water; an overlapping chain of ripples swung back from it. At approximately the middle of the pond, the depression became a commotion. A small whirlpool formed and died, and the ripples began to settle.

"There's your ghost, Bert," Gregory gasped. "That must have been the one that got poor Mrs. Grendon. Now do you believe?"

"I never heard of a ghost as lived under water," Neckland gasped.

"A ghost never harmed anyone—we've already had a sample of what these terrifying things can do. Come on, Bert, shake hands, understand I bear you no hard feelings. Oh, come on, man! I know how you feel about Nancy, but she must be free to make her own choice in life."

They shook hands and grinned rather foolishly at each other.

"We better go and tell the farmer what we seen," Neckland said. "I reckon that thing done what happened to Lardie last evening."

"Lardie? What's happened to her? I thought I hadn't seen her today."

"Same as happened to the little pigs. I found her just inside the barn. Just her coat was left, that's all. No insides! Like she'd been sucked dry."

"Let's go, Bert."

* * *

It took Gregory twenty minutes to summon the council of war on which he had set his mind. The party gathered in the farmhouse, in the parlour. By this time, Nancy had somewhat recovered from the shock of her mother's death, and sat in an armchair with a shawl about her shoulders. Her father stood nearby with his arms folded, looking impatient, while Bert Neckland lounged by the door. Only Grubby was not present. He had been told to get on with the ditching.

"I'm going to have another attempt to convince you all that you are in very grave danger," Gregory said. "You won't see it for yourselves, so I—"

He paused. There was a dragging noise on the landing upstairs, a board creaked.

"Who the devil's up there?" Grendon growled. He made towards the stairwell.

"Don't go, father!" Nancy screamed, but her father flung open the door and made his way up. Gregory bit his lip. The Aurigans had never ventured into the house before.

In a moment, Grendon returned with a monstrous piglet in his arms.

"Keep the confounded animals out of the house, Nancy," he said, pushing the creature squealing out of the front door.

The interruption made Gregory realize how his nerves still jangled. He set his back to the sawdust-filled parody of a goat that watched from its case, and spoke quickly.

"The situation is that we're all animals together at present. Do you remember that strange meteor that fell out of the sky last winter, Joseph? And do you remember that ill-smelling dew early in the spring? They were not unconnected, and they are connected with all that's happening now. That meteor was a space machine of some sort, I firmly believe, and it brought in it a kind of life that—that is not so much hostile to terrestrial life as *indifferent to its quality.*

The creatures from that machine—I call them Aurigans—spread the dew over the farm. It was a growth accelerator, a manure or fertilizer, that speeds growth in plants and animals."

"So much better for us!" Grendon said.

"But it's not better. The things grow wildly, yes, but the taste is altered to suit the palates of those things out there. You've seen what happened. You can't sell anything. People won't touch your eggs or milk or meat—they taste too foul."

"But that's a lot of nonsense. We'll sell in Norwich. Our produce is better than it ever was. We eat it, don't we?"

"Yes, Joseph, *you* eat it. But anyone who eats at your table is doomed. Don't you understand—you are all 'fertilized' just as surely as the pigs and chickens. Your place has been turned into a superfarm, and you are all meat to the Aurigans."

That set a silence in the room, until Nancy said in a small voice, "You don't believe such a terrible thing."

"I suppose these unseen creatures told you all this?" Grendon said truculently.

"Judge by the evidence, as I do. Your wife—I must be brutal, Joseph—your wife was eaten, like the dog and the pigs. As everything else will be in time. The Aurigans aren't even cannibals. They aren't like us. They don't care whether we have souls or intelligences, any more than we really care whether the bullocks have."

"No one's going to eat me," Neckland said, looking decidedly white about the gills.

"How can you stop them? They're invisible, and I think they can strike like snakes. They're aquatic and I think they may be only two feet tall. How can you protect yourself?" He turned to the farmer. "Joseph, the danger is very great, and not only to us here. At first, they may have offered us no harm while they got the measure of us—otherwise I'd have died in

your rowing boat. Now there's no longer doubt of their hostile intent. I beg you to let me go to Heigham and telephone to the chief of police in Norwich, or at least to the local militia, to get them to come and help us."

The farmer shook his head slowly, and pointed a finger at Gregory.

"You soon forgot them talks we had, bor, all about the coming age of socialism and how the powers of the state was going to wither away. Directly we get a bit of trouble, you want to call in the authorities. There's no harm here a few savage dogs like my old Cuff can't handle, and I don't say as I ent going to get a couple of dogs, but you'm a fule if you reckon I'm getting the authorities down here. Fine old socialist you turn out to be!"

"You have no room to talk about that!" Gregory exclaimed. "Why didn't you let Grubby come here? If you were a socialist, you'd treat the men as you treat yourself. Instead, you leave him out in the ditch. I wanted him to hear this discussion."

The farmer leant threateningly across the table at him.

"Oh, you did, did you? Since when was this your farm? And Grubby can come and go as he likes when it's his, so put that in your pipe and smoke it, bor! Who do you just think you are?" He moved closer to Gregory, apparently happy to work off his fears as anger. "You'm trying to scare us all off this here little old bit of ground, ent you? Well, the Grendons ent a scaring sort, see! Now I'll tell you something. See that rifle there on the wall? That be loaded. And if you ent off this farm by midday, that rifle ont be on that wall no more. It'll be here, bor, right here in my two hands, and I'll be letting you have it right where you'll feel it most."

"You can't do that, father," Nancy said. "You know Gregory is a friend of ours."

"For God's sake, Joseph," Gregory said, "see where your enemy lies. Bert, tell Mr. Grendon what we saw on the pond, go on."

Neckland was far from keen to be dragged into this argument. He scratched his head, drew a red-and-white spotted kerchief from round his neck to wipe his face, and muttered, "We saw a sort of ripple on the water, but I didn't see nothing really, Master Gregory. I meant, it could have been the wind, couldn't it?"

"Now you be warned, Gregory," the farmer repeated. "You be off my land by noon by the sun, and that mare of yours, or I ont answer for it." He marched out into the pale sunshine, and Neckland followed.

Nancy and Gregory stood staring at each other. He took her hands, and they were cold.

"You believe what I was saying, Nancy?"

"Is that why the food did at one point taste bad to us, and then soon tasted well enough again?"

"It can only have been that at that time your systems were not fully adjusted to the poison. Now they are. You're being fed up, Nancy, just like the livestock—I'm sure of it! I fear for you, darling love, I fear so much. What are we to do? Come back to Cottersall with me! Mrs. Fenn has another fine little drawing-room upstairs that I'm sure she would rent."

"Now you're talking nonsense, Greg! How can I? What would people say? No, you go away for now and let the tempest of father's wrath abate, and if you could come back tomorrow, you will find he will be milder for sure, because I plan to wait on him tonight and talk to him about you. Why, he's half daft with grief and doesn't know what he says."

"All right, my darling. But stay inside as much as you can. The Aurigans have not come indoors yet, as far as we know, and it may be safer here. And lock all

the doors and put the shutters over the windows before you go to bed. And get your father to take that rifle of his upstairs with him."

The evenings were lengthening with confidence towards summer now, and Bruce Fox arrived home before sunset. As he jumped from his bicycle this evening, he found his friend Gregory impatiently awaiting him.

They went indoors together, and while Fox ate a large tea, Gregory told him what had been happening at the farm that day.

"You're in trouble," Fox said. "Look, tomorrow's Sunday. I'll skip church and come out with you. You need help."

"Joseph may shoot me. He'll be certain to if I bring along a stranger. You can help me tonight by telling me where I can purchase a young dog straight away to protect Nancy."

"Nonsense, I'm coming with you. I can't bear hearing all this at second hand anyhow. We'll pick up a pup in any event—the blacksmith has a litter to be rid of. Have you got any plan of action?"

"Plan? No, not really."

"You must have a plan. Grendon doesn't scare too easily, does he?"

"I imagine he's scared well enough. Nancy says he's scared. He just isn't imaginative enough to see what he can do but carry on working as hard as possible."

"Look, I know these farmers. They won't believe anything till you rub their noses in it. What we must do is *show* him an Aurigan."

"Oh, splendid, Bruce! And how do you catch one?"

"You trap one."

"Don't forget they're invisible—hey, Bruce, yes, by Jove, you're right! I've the very idea! Look, we've

nothing more to worry about if we can trap one. We can trap the lot, however many there are, and we can kill the little horrors when we have trapped them."

Fox grinned over the top of a chunk of cherry cake. "We're agreed, I suppose, that these Aurigans aren't socialist utopians any longer?"

It helped a great deal, Gregory thought, to be able to visualize roughly what the alien life form looked like. The volume on serpents had been a happy find, for not only did it give an idea of how the Aurigans must be able to digest their prey so rapidly—"a kind of soup or broth"—but presumably it gave a clue to their appearance. To live in a space machine, they would probably be fairly small, and they seemed to be semi-aquatic. It all went to make up a picture of a strange being: skin perhaps scaled like a fish, great flipper feet like a frog, barrel-like diminutive stature, and a tiny head with two great fangs in the jaw. There was no doubt that the invisibility cloaked a really ugly-looking dwarf!

As the macabre image passed through his head, Gregory and Bruce Fox were preparing their trap. Fortunately, Grendon had offered no resistance to their entering the farm; Nancy had evidently spoken to good effect. And he had suffered another shock. Five fowls had been reduced to little but feathers and skin that morning almost before his eyes, and he was as a result sullen and indifferent to what went on. Now he was out in a distant field, working, and the two young men were allowed to carry out their plans unmolested—though not without an occasional anxious glance at the pond—while a worried Nancy looked on from the farmhouse window.

She had with her a sturdy young mongrel dog of eight months, which Gregory and Bruce had brought along, called Gyp. Grendon had obtained two ferocious hounds from a distant neighbour. These wide-

mouthed brutes were secured on long running chains that enabled them to patrol from the horse trough by the pond, down the west side of the house, almost to the elms and the bridge leading over to West Field. They barked stridently most of the time and seemed to cause a general unease among the other animals, all of which gave voice restlessly this forenoon.

The dogs would be a difficulty, Nancy had said, for they refused to touch any of the food the farm could provide. It was hoped they would take it when they became hungry enough.

Grendon had planted a great board by the farm gate and on the board had painted a notice telling everyone to keep away.

Armed with pitchforks, the two young men carried flour sacks out from the mill and placed them at strategic positions across the yard as far as the gate. Gregory went to the cowsheds and let out one of the calves there on a length of binder twine under the very teeth of the barking dogs—he only hoped they would prove as hostile to the Aurigans as they seemed to be to human life.

As he was pulling the calf across the yard, Grubby appeared.

"You'd better stay away from us, Grubby. We're trying to trap one of the ghosts."

"Master, if I catch one, I shall strangle him, straight I will."

"A pitchfork is a better weapon. These ghosts are dangerous little beasts at close quarters."

"I'm strong, bor, I tell 'ee! I'd strangle un!"

To prove his point, Grubby rolled his striped and tattered sleeve even further up his arm and exposed to Gregory and Fox his enormous biceps. At the same time, he wagged his great heavy head and lolled his tongue out of his mouth, perhaps to demonstrate some of the effects of strangulation.

"It's a very fine arm," Gregory agreed. "But look,

Grubby, we have a better idea. We are going to do this ghost to death with pitchforks; if you want to join in, you'd better get a spare one from the stable."

Grubby looked at him with a sly-shy expression and stroked his throat. "I'd be better at strangling, bor. I've always wanted to strangle someone."

"Why should you want to do that, Grubby?"

The labourer lowered his voice. "I always wanted to see how difficult it would be. I'm strong, you see. I got my strength up as a lad doing some of this here strangling—but never men, you know, just cattle."

Backing away a pace, Gregory said, "This time, Grubby, it's pitchforks for us." To settle the issue, he went into the stables, got a pitchfork, and returned to thrust it into Grubby's hand.

"Let's get on with it," Fox said.

They were all ready to start. Fox and Grubby crouched down in the ditch on either side of the gate, weapons at the ready. Gregory emptied one of the bags of flour over the yard in a patch just before the gate, so that anyone leaving the farm would have to walk through it. Then he led the calf towards the pond.

The young animal set up an uneasy mooing, and most of the beasts nearby seemed to answer. The chickens and hens scattered about the yard in the pale sunshine as if demented. Gregory felt the sweat trickle down his back, although his skin was cold with the chemistries of suspense. With a slap on its rump, he forced the calf into the water of the pond. It stood there unhappily, until he led it out again and slowly back across the yard, past the mill and the grain store on his right, past Mrs. Grendon's neglected flowerbed on his left, towards the gate where his allies waited. And for all his determination not to do so, he could not stop himself looking backwards at the leaden surface of the pond to see if anything followed him. He led the calf through the gate and

stopped. No tracks but his and the calf's showed in the strewn flour.

"Try it again," Fox advised. "Perhaps they are taking a nap down there."

Gregory went through the routine again, and a third and fourth time, on each occasion smoothing the flour after he had been through it. Each time, he saw Nancy watching helplessly from the house. Each time, he felt a little more sick with tension.

Yet when it happened, it took him by surprise. He had got the calf to the gate for a fifth time when Fox's shout joined the chorus of animal noises. The pond had shown no special ripple, so the Aurigan had come from some dark-purposed prowl of the farm—suddenly, its finned footsteps were marking the flour.

Yelling with excitement, Gregory dropped the rope that led the calf and ducked to one side. Seizing up an opened bag of flour by the gatepost, he flung its contents before the advancing figure.

The bomb of flour exploded all over the Aurigan. Now it was revealed in chalky outline. Despite himself, Gregory found himself screaming in sheer fright as the ghastliness was revealed in whirling white. It was especially the size that frightened: this dread thing, remote from human form, was too big for earthly nature—ten feet high, perhaps twelve! Invincible, and horribly quick, it came rushing at him with unnumbered arms striking out towards him.

Next morning, Dr. Crouchorn and his silk hat appeared at Gregory's bedside, thanked Mrs. Fenn for some hot water, and dressed Gregory's leg wound.

"You got off lightly, considering," the old man said. "But if you will take a piece of advice from me, Mr. Rolles, you will cease to visit the Grendon farm.

It's an evil place and you'll come to no good there."

Gregory nodded. He had told the doctor nothing, except that Grendon had run up and shot him in the leg; which was true enough, but that it omitted most of the story.

"When will I be up again, Doctor?"

"Oh, young flesh heals soon enough, or undertakers would be rich men and doctors paupers. A few days should see you right as rain. But I'll be visiting you again tomorrow, until when you are to stay flat on your back and keep that leg motionless."

"I understand."

The doctor made a ferocious face. "You understand, but will you take heed? I'm warning you, if you take one step on that leg, it will turn purple and fall off." He nodded slowly and emphatically, and the lines on his face deepened to such a great extent that anyone familiar with the eccentricities of his physiognomy would be inclined to estimate that he was smiling.

"I suppose I may write a letter, doctor?"

"I suppose you may, young man."

Directly Dr. Crouchorn had gone, Gregory took pen and paper and addressed some urgent lines to Nancy. They told her that he loved her very much and could not bear to think of her remaining on the farm; that he could not get to see her for a few days because of his leg wound; and that she must immediately come away on Hetty with a bag full of her things and stay at "The Wayfarer," where there was a capital room for which he would pay. That if she thought anything of him, she must put the simple plan into action this very day, and send him word round from the inn when she was established there.

With some satisfaction, Gregory read this through twice, signed it and added kisses, and summoned Mrs. Fenn with the aid of a small bell she had provided for that purpose.

He told her that the delivery of the letter was a matter of extreme urgency. He would entrust it to Tommy, the baker's boy, to deliver when his morning round was over, and would give him a shilling for his efforts. Mrs. Fenn was not enthusiastic about this, but with a little flattery was persuaded to speak to Tommy; she left the bedroom clutching both letter and shilling.

At once, Gregory began a letter, this one to Mr. H. G. Wells. It was some while since he had last addressed his correspondent, and so he had to make a somewhat lengthy report; but eventually he came to the events of the previous day.

"So horrified was I by the sight of the Aurigan (he wrote), that I stood where I was, unable to move, while the flour blew about us. And how can I now convey to you—who are perhaps the most interested person in this vital subject in all the British Isles—what the monster looked like, outlined in white? My impressions were, of course, both brief and indefinite, but the main handicap is that there is nothing on Earth to liken this weird being to!

"It appeared, I suppose, most like some horrendous goose, but the neck must be imagined as almost as thick as the body—indeed, it was almost all body, or all neck, whichever way you look at it. And on top of this neck was no head but a terrible array of various sorts of arms, a nest of writhing cilia, antennae, and whips, for all the world as if an octopus were entangled with a Portuguese Man-o'-war as big as itself, with a few shrimp and starfish legs thrown in. Does this sound ludicrous? I can only swear to you that as it bore down on me, perhaps twice my own height or more, I found it something almost too terrifying for human eyes to look on—and yet I did not see it, but merely the flour that adhered to it!

"That repulsive sight would have been the last my

eyes ever dwelt on had it not been for Grubby, the simple farmhand I have had occasion to mention before.

"As I threw the flour, Grubby gave a great cry and rushed forward, dropping the pitchfork. He jumped at the creature as it turned on me. This put out our plan, which was that he and Bruce Fox should pitchfork the creature to death. Instead, he grasped it as high as he possibly might and commenced to squeeze with the full force of his mighty muscles. What a terrifying contest! What a fear-fraught combat!

"Collecting his wits, Bruce charged forward and attacked with his pitchfork. It was his battle cry that brought me back from my paralysis into action. I ran and seized Grubby's pitchfork and also charged. That thing had arms for us all! It struck out, and I have no doubt now that several arms held poisoned needle teeth, for I saw one come towards me gaping like a snake's mouth. Need I stress the danger—particularly when you recall that the effect of the flour cloud was only partial, and there were still invisible arms flailing round us!

"Our saving was that the Aurigan was cowardly. I saw Bruce jab it hard, and a second later, I rammed my pitchfork right through its foot. At once it had had enough. Grubby fell to the ground as it retreated. It moved at amazing speed, back towards the pool. We were in pursuit! And all the beasts of the barnyard uttered their cries to it.

"As it launched itself into the water, we both flung our pitchforks at its form. But it swam out strongly and then dived below the surface, leaving only ripples and a scummy trail of flour.

"We stood staring at the water for an instant, and then with common accord ran back to Grubby. He was dead. He lay face up and was no longer recognizable. The Aurigan must have struck him with its

poisoned fangs as soon as he attacked. Grubby's skin was stretched tight and glistened oddly. He had turned a dull crimson. All his internal substance had been transformed to liquid by the rapid-working venoms of the Aurigan; he was like a sort of giant man-shaped rotten haggis.

"There were wound marks across his neck and throat and what had been his face, and from these wounds his substance drained, so that he slowly deflated into his trampled bed of flour and dust. Perhaps the sight of fabled Medusa's head, that turned men to stone, was no worse than this, for we stood there utterly paralyzed. It was a blast from Farmer Grendon's rifle that brought us back to life.

"He had threatened to shoot me. Now, seeing us despoiling his flour stocks and apparently about to make off with a calf, he fired at us. We had no choice but to run for it. Grendon was in no explaining mood. Good Nancy came running out to stop him, but Neckland was charging up too with the pair of savage dogs growling at the end of their chains.

"Bruce and I had ridden up on my Daisy. I had left her saddled. Bringing her out of the stable at a trot, I heaved Bruce up into the saddle and was about to climb on myself when the gun went off again and I felt a burning pain in my leg. Bruce dragged me into the saddle and we were off—I half unconscious.

"Here I lie now in bed, and should be about again in a couple of days. Fortunately, the shot did not harm any bones.

"So you see how the farm is now a place of the damned! Once, I thought it might even become a new Eden, growing the food of the gods for men like gods. Instead—alas! the first meeting between humanity and beings from another world has proved disastrous, and the Eden is become a battleground for a war of worlds. How can our anticipations for the future be anything other than gloomy?

"Before I close this over-long account, I must

answer a query in your letter and pose another to you, more personal than yours to me.

"First, you question if the Aurigans are entirely invisible and say—if I may quote your letter—'Any alteration in the refractive index of the eye lenses would make vision impossible, but without such alteration the eyes would be visible as glassy globules. And for vision it is also necessary that there should be visual purple behind the retina and an opaque cornea. How then do your Aurigans manage for vision?' The answer must be that they do without eyesight as we know it, for I think they naturally maintain a complete invisibility. How they 'see' I know not, but whatever sense they use, it is effective. How they communicate I know not—our fellow made not the slightest sound when I speared his foot!—yet it is apparent they must communicate effectively. Perhaps they tried originally to communicate with us through a mysterious sense we do not possess and, on receiving no answer, assumed us to be as dumb as our dumb animals. If so, what a tragedy!

"Now to my personal enquiry. I know, sir, that you must grow more busy as you grow more famous; but I feel that what transpires here in this remote corner of East Anglia is of momentous import to the world and the future. Could you not take it upon yourself to pay us a visit here? You would be comfortable at one of our two inns, and the journey here by railway is efficient if tedious—you can easily get a regular waggon from Heigham station here, a distance of only eight miles. You could then view Grendon's farm for yourself, and perhaps one of these interstellar beings too. I feel you are as much amused as concerned by the accounts you receive from the undersigned, but I swear not one detail is exaggerated. Say you can come!

"If you need persuasion, reflect on how much delight it will give to:

"Your sincere admirer and friend,
GREGORY ROLLES."

Reading this long letter through, scratching out two superfluous adjectives, Gregory lay back in some satisfaction. He had the feeling he was still involved in the struggle although temporarily out of action.

But the late afternoon brought him disquieting news. Tommy, the baker's boy, had gone out as far as the Grendon farm. Then the ugly legends circulating in the village about the place had risen in his mind, and he had stood wondering whether he should go on. An unnatural babble of animal noise came from the farm, mixed with hammering, and when Tommy crept forward and saw the farmer himself looking as black as a puddle and building a great thing like a gibbet in the yard, he had lost his nerve and rushed back the way he came, the letter to Nancy undelivered.

Bruce Fox arrived that evening to see how his friend was, and Gregory tried to persuade him to take the letter. But Fox was able successfully to plead a prior engagement. They talked for a while, mainly running over the horrors of the previous day once more, and then Fox left.

Gregory lay on the bed worrying about Nancy until Mrs. Fenn brought up supper on a tray. At least it was clear now why the Aurigans had not entered the farmhouse; they were far too large to do so. She was safe as long as she kept indoors—as far as anyone on that doomed plot was safe.

He fell asleep early that night. In the early hours of the morning, nightmare visited him. He was in a strange city where all the buildings were new and the people wore shining clothes. In one square grew a tree. The Gregory in the dream stood in a special relationship to the tree: he fed it. It was his job to push people who were passing by the tree against its surface. The tree was a saliva tree. Down its smooth

bark ran quantities of saliva from red lips like leaves up in the boughs. It grew enormous on the people on which it fed. As they were thrown against it, they passed into the substance of the tree. Some of the saliva splashed on to Gregory. But instead of dissolving him, it caused everything he touched to be dissolved. He put his arms about the girl he loved, and as his mouth went towards hers, her skin peeled away from her face.

He woke weeping desperately and fumbling blindly for the ring of the gas mantle.

Dr. Crouchorn came late next morning and told Gregory he should have at least three more days complete rest for the recovery of the muscles of his leg. Gregory lay there in a state of acute dissatisfaction with himself. Recalling the vile dream, he thought how negligent he had been towards Nancy, the girl he loved. His letter to her still lay undelivered by his bedside. After Mrs. Fenn had brought up his dinner, he determined that he must see Nancy for himself. Leaving the food, he pulled himself out of bed and dressed slowly.

The leg was more painful than he had expected, but he got himself downstairs and out to the stable without too much trouble. Daisy seemed pleased to see him. He rubbed her nose and rested his head against her long cheek in sheer pleasure at being with her again.

"This may be the last time you have to undertake this particular journey, my girl," he said.

Saddling her was comparatively easy. Getting into the saddle involved much bodily anguish. But eventually he was comfortable and they turned along the familiar and desolate road to the domain of the Aurigans. His leg was worse than he had bargained for. More than once, he had to get the mare to stop while he let the throbbing subside. He saw he was losing blood plentifully.

As he approached the farm, he observed what the baker's boy had meant by saying Grendon was building a gibbet. A pole had been set up in the middle of the yard. A cable ran to the top of it and a light was rigged there, so that the expanse of the yard could be illuminated by night.

Another change had taken place. A wooden fence had been built behind the horse trough, cutting off the pond from the farm. But at one point, ominously, a section of it had been broken down and splintered and crushed, as if some monstrous thing had walked through the barrier unheeding.

A ferocious dog was chained just inside the gate, and barking its head off, to the consternation of the poultry. Gregory dare not enter. As he stood pondering the best way to tackle this fresh problem, the door of the farmhouse opened fractionally and Nancy peeped out. He called and signalled frantically to her.

Timidly, she ran across and let him in, dragging the dog back. Gregory hitched Daisy to the gatepost and kissed her cheek, soothed by the feel of her sturdy body in his arms.

"Where's your father?"

"My dearest, your leg, your poor leg! It's bleeding yet!"

"Never mind my leg. Where's your father?"

"He's down in South Meadow, I think."

"Good! I'm going to speak with him. Nancy, I want you to go indoors and pack some belongings. I'm taking you away with me."

"I can't leave father!"

"You must. I'm going to tell him now." As he limped across the yard, she called fearfully, "He has that there gun of his'n with him all the time—do be careful!"

The two dogs on a running chain followed him all the way down the side of the house, nearly choking

in their efforts to get at him, their teeth flashing uncomfortably close to his ankles.

Near the elms, he saw that several wild birds lay in the grass. One was still fluttering feebly. He could only assume they had worn themselves out trying to feed their immense and hungry broods. Which was what would happen to the farmer in time, he reflected. He noticed Neckland below Grubby's little hut, busy sawing wood; the farmer was not with him. On impulse, Gregory turned into the sties.

It was gloomy there. In the gloom, Grendon worked. He dropped his bucket when he saw Gregory there, and came forward threateningly.

"You come back? Why don't you stay away? Can't you see the notice by the gate? I don't want you here no more, bor. I know you mean well, and I intend you no harm, but I'll kee 'ee, understand, kill 'ee if you ever come here again. I've plenty of worries without you to add to them. Now then, get you going!"

Gregory stood his ground.

"Mr. Grendon, are you as mad as your wife was before she died? Do you understand that you may meet Grubby's fate at any moment? Do you realize what you are harbouring in your pond?"

"I ent a fule. But suppose them there things do eat everything, humans included? Suppose this is now their farm? They still got to have someone tend it. So I reckon they ent going to harm me. So long as they sees me work hard, they ent going to harm me."

"You're being fattened, do you understand? For all the hard work you do, you must have put on a stone this last month. Doesn't that scare you?"

Something of the farmer's pose broke for a moment. He cast a wild look round. "I ent saying I ent scared. I'm saying I'm doing what I have to do. We don't own our lives. Now do me a favour and get out of here."

Instinctively, Gregory's glance had followed Grendon's. For the first time, he saw in the dimness the size of the pigs. Their great broad black backs were visible over the top of the sties. They were the size of young oxen.

"This is a farm of death," he said.

"Death's always the end of all of us, pig or cow or man alike."

"Right-ho, Mr. Grendon, you can think like that if you like. It's not my way of thinking, nor am I going to see your dependants suffer from your madness. Mr. Grendon, sir, I wish to ask for your daughter's hand in marriage."

For the first three days that she was away from her home, Nancy Grendon lay in her room in "The Wayfarer" near to death. It seemed as if all ordinary food poisoned her. But gradually under Doctor Crouchorn's ministration—terrified perhaps by the rage she suspected he would vent upon her should she fail to get better—she recovered her strength.

"You look so much better today," Gregory said, clasping her hand. "You'll soon be up and about again, once your system is free of all the evil nourishment of the farm."

"Greg, dearest, promise me you will not go to the farm again. You have no need to go now I'm not there."

He cast his eyes down and said, "Then you don't have to get me to promise, do you?"

"I just want to be sure we neither of us go there again. Father, I feel sure, bears a charmed life. But I—I feel now as if I'm waking from a nightmare!"

"Don't think about it! Look, I've brought you some flowers!"

He produced a clay pot overloaded with wallflowers with gigantic blooms and gave it to her.

She smiled and said, "They're so large! Greg—

they're—they're from the farm, aren't they? They're unnaturally large."

"I thought you'd like a souvenir of the nicer side of your home."

With all her strength, she hurled the pot across the room. It struck the door and broke. The dark earth scattered over the boards and the flowers lay broken on the floor.

"You dare bring the curse in here! And, Greg, this means you've been back to the farm, doesn't it, since we come away together?"

He nodded his head, looking defiantly at her. "I had to see what was happening."

"Please don't go there again, Greg, please. It's as if I was now coming to my senses again—but I don't want it to be as if you was losing yours! Supposing those things followed us here to Cottersall, those Aurigans?"

"You know, Nancy, I've wondered several times why they remain on the farm as they do. You would think that once they found they could so easily defeat human beings, they would attack everyone, or send for more of their own kind and try to invade us. Yet they seem perfectly content to remain in that one small space."

She smiled. "I may not be very clever compared with you, but I tell 'ee the answer to that one. They ent interested in going anywhere. I think there's just two of them, and they come to our little old world for a holiday in their space machine, same as we might go to Great Yarmouth for a couple of days for our honeymoon. Perhaps they're on their honeymoon."

"On honeymoon! What a ghastly idea!"

"Well, on holiday then. That was father's idea—he says as there's just two of them, treating Earth as a quiet place to stay. People like to eat well when they're on holiday, don't they?"

He stared at Nancy aghast.

"But that's horrible! You're trying to make the Aurigans out to be *pleasant*!"

"Of course I ent, you silly ha'p'orth! But I expect they seem pleasant to each other."

"Well, I prefer to think of them as menaces."

"All the more reason for you to keep away from them!"

But to be out of sight was not to be out of mind's reach. Gregory received another letter from Dr. Hudson-Ward, a kind and encouraging one, but he made no attempt to answer it. He felt he could not bear to take up any work that would remove him from the neighbourhood, although the need to work, in view of his matrimonial plans, was now pressing; the modest allowance his father made him would not support two in any comfort. Yet he could not bring his thought to grapple with such practical problems. It was another letter he looked for, and the horrors of the farm that obsessed him. And the next night, he dreamed of the saliva tree again.

In the evening, he plucked up enough courage to tell Fox and Nancy about it. They met in the little snug at the back of "The Wayfarer's" public bars, a discreet and private place with red plush on the seats. Nancy was her usual self again, and had been out for a brief walk in the afternoon sunshine.

"People wanted to give themselves to the saliva tree. And although I didn't see this for myself, I had the distinct feeling that perhaps they weren't actually killed so much as changed into something else—something less human maybe. And this time, I saw the tree was made of metal of some kind and was growing bigger and bigger by pumps—you could see through the saliva tree to big armatures and pistons, and out of the branches steam was pouring."

Fox laughed, a little unsympathetically. "Sounds to me like the shape of things to come, when even plants are grown by machinery. Events are preying on your mind, Greg! Listen, my sister is going to

Norwich tomorrow, driving in her uncle's trap. Why don't the two of you go with her? She's going to buy some adornments for her bridal gown, so that should interest you, Nancy. Then you could stay with Greg's uncle for a couple of days. I assure you I will let you know immediately the Aurigans invade Cottersall, so you won't miss anything."

Nancy seized Gregory's arm. "Can we please, Gregory, can we? I ent been to Norwich for long enough and it's a fine city."

"It would be a good idea," he said doubtfully.

Both of them pressed him until he was forced to yield. He broke up the little party as soon as he decently could, kissed Nancy goodnight, and walked hurriedly back down the street to the baker's. Of one thing he was certain: if he must leave the district even for a short while, he had to have a look to see what was happening at the farm before he went.

The farm looked in the summer's dusk as it had never done before. Massive wooden screens nine feet high had been erected and hastily creosoted. They stood about in forlorn fashion, intended to keep the public gaze from the farm, but lending it unmeaning. They stood not only in the yard but at irregular intervals along the boundaries of the land, inappropriately among fruit trees, desolately amid bracken, irrelevantly in swamp. A sound of furious hammering, punctuated by the unwearying animal noises, indicated that more screens were still being built.

But what lent the place its unearthly look was the lighting. The solitary pole supporting electric light now had five companions: one by the gate, one by the pond, one behind the house, one outside the engine house, one down by the pigsties. Their hideous yellow glare reduced the scene to the sort of unlikely picture that might be found and puzzled over in the eternal midnight of an Egyptian tomb.

Gregory was too wise to try and enter by the gate.

He hitched Daisy to the low branches of a thorn tree and set off over waste land, entering Grendon's property by the South Meadow. As he walked stealthily towards the distant outhouses, he could see how the farm land differed from the territory about it. The corn was already so high it seemed in the dark almost to threaten by its ceaseless whisper of movement. The fruits had ripened fast. In the strawberry beds were great strawberries like pears. The marrows lay on their dunghill like bloated bolsters, gleaming from a distant shaft of light. In the orchard, the trees creaked, weighed down by distorted footballs that passed for apples; with a heavy autumnal thud one fell over-ripe to the ground. Everywhere on the farm, there seemed to be slight movement and noise, so much so that Gregory stopped to listen.

A wind was rising. The sails of the old mill shrieked like a gull's cry as they began to turn. In the engine house, the steam engine pumped out its double unfaltering note as it generated power. The dogs still raged, the animals added their uneasy chorus. He recalled the saliva tree; here as in the dream, it was as if agriculture had become industry, and the impulses of nature swallowed by the new god of Science. In the bark of the trees rose the dark steam of novel and unknown forces.

He talked himself into pressing forward again. He moved carefully through the baffling slices of shadow and illumination created by the screens and lights, and arrived near the back door of the farmhouse. A lantern burnt in the kitchen window. As Gregory hesitated, the crunch of broken glass came from within.

Cautiously, he edged himself past the window and peered in through the doorway. From the parlour, he heard the voice of Grendon. It held a curious muffled tone, as if the man spoke to himself.

"Lie there! You're no use to me. This is a trial of strength. Oh God, preserve me, to let me prove

myself! Thou has made my land barren till now—now let me harvest it! I don't know what You're doing. I didn't mean to presume, but this here farm is my life. Curse 'em, curse 'em all! They're all enemies." There was more of it; the man was muttering like one drunk. With a horrid fascination, Gregory was drawn forward till he had crossed the kitchen flags and stood on the verge of the larger room. He peered round the half open door until he could see the farmer, standing obscurely in the middle of the room.

A candle stood in the neglected hearth, its flickering flame glassily reflected in the cases of maladroit animals. Evidently the house electricity had been cut to give additional power to the new lights outside.

Grendon's back was to Gregory. One gaunt and unshaven cheek was lit by candle-light. His back seemed a little bent by the weight of what he imagined his duties, yet looking at that leather-clad back now Gregory experienced a sort of reverence for the independence of the man, and for the mystery that lay under his plainness. He watched as Grendon moved out through the front door, leaving it hanging wide, and passed into the yard, still muttering to himself. He walked round the side of the house and was hidden from view as the sound of his tread was lost amid the renewed barking of dogs.

The tumult did not drown a groan from near at hand. Peering into the shadows, Gregory saw a body lying under the table. It rolled over, crunching broken glass as it did so, and exclaimed in a dazed way. Without being able to see clearly, Gregory knew it was Neckland. He climbed over to the man and propped his head up, kicking away a stuffed fish as he did so.

"Don't kill me, bor! I only want to get away from here. I only want to get away."

"Bert? It's Greg here. Bert, are you badly hurt?"

He could see some wounds. The fellow's shirt had

been practically torn from his back, and the flesh on his side and back was cut from where he had rolled in the glass. More serious was a great weal over one shoulder, changing to a deeper colour as Gregory looked at it. A brawl had taken place. Under the table lay another fish, its mouth gaping as if it still died, and the pseudo-goat, one button eye of which had rolled out of its socket. The cases from which they had come lay shattered by the wall.

Wiping his face and speaking in a more rational voice, Neckland said, "Gregory? I thought as you was down Cottersall? What you doing here? He'll kill you proper if he finds you here!"

"What happened to you, Bert? Can you get up?"

The labourer was again in possession of his faculties. He grabbed Gregory's forearm and said imploringly, "Keep your voice down, for Christ's sake, or he'll hear us and come back and settle my hash for once for all! He's gone clean off his head, says as these pond things are having a holiday here. He nearly knocked my head off my shoulder with that stick of his! Lucky I got a thick head!"

"What was the quarrel about?"

"I tell you straight, bor, I have got the wind up proper about this here farm. They things as live in the pond will eat me and suck me up like they done Grubby if I stay here any more. So I run off when Joe Grendon weren't looking, and I come in here to gather up my traps and my bits and leave here at once. This whole place is evil, a bed of evil, and it ought to be destroyed. Hell can't be worse than this here farm!"

"So he caught you in here, did he?"

"I saw him rush in and I flung that there fish at him, and the goat. But he had me! Now I'm getting out, and I'd advise you to do the same. You must be daft, come back here like you did!"

As he spoke, he pulled himself to his feet and stood, keeping his balance with Gregory's aid.

Grunting, he made his way over the staircase.

"Bert," Gregory said, "supposing we rush Grendon and lay him out. We can then get him in the cart and all leave together."

Neckland turned to stare at him, his face hidden in shadows, nursing his shoulder with one hand.

"You try it!" he said, and then he turned and went steadily up the stairs.

Gregory stood where he was, keeping one eye on the window. He had come to the farm without any clear notion in his head, but now that the idea had been formulated, he saw that it was up to him to try and remove Grendon from his farm. He felt obliged to do it; for although he had lost his former regard for Grendon, a sort of fascination for the man held him, and he was incapable of leaving any human being, however perverse, to face alone the alien horrors of the farm. It occurred to him that he might get help from the distant houses, Dereham Cottages, if only the farmer were rendered in one way or another unable to pepper the intruders with shot.

The machine house possessed only one high window, and that was barred. It was built of brick and had a stout door which could be barred and locked from outside. Perhaps it would be possible to lure Grendon into there; outside aid could then be obtained.

Not without apprehension, Gregory went to the open door and peered out into the confused dark. He stared anxiously at the ground for sight of a footstep more sinister than the farmer's, but there was no indication that the Aurigans were active. He stepped into the yard.

He had not gone two yards before a woman's screams rang out. The sound seemed to clamp an icy grip about Gregory's ribs, and into his mind came a picture of poor mad Mrs. Grendon. Then he recognized the voice, in its few shouted words, as Nancy's. Even before the sound cut off, he began to pelt down

the dark side of the house as fast as he could run.

Only later did he realize how he seemed to be running against a great army of animal cries. Loudest was the babel of the pigs; every swine seemed to have some message deep and nervous and indecipherable to deliver to an unknown source; and it was to the sties that Gregory ran, swerving past the giant screens under the high and sickly light.

The noise in the sties was deafening. Every animal was attacking its pen with its sharp hooves. One light swung over the middle pen. With its help, Gregory saw immediately how terrible was the change that had come over the farm since his last visit. The sows had swollen enormously and their great ears clattered against their cheeks like boards. Their hirsute backs curved almost to the rafters of their prison.

Grendon was at the far entrance. In his arms he held the unconscious form of his daughter. A sack of pig feed lay scattered by his feet. He had one pen gate half open and was trying to thrust his way in against the flank of a pig whose mighty shoulder came almost level with his. He turned and stared at Gregory with a face whose blankness was more terrifying than any expression of rage.

There was another presence in the place. A pen gate near to Gregory swung open. The two sows wedged in the narrow sty gave out a terrible falsetto squealing, clearly scenting the presence of an unappeasable hunger. They kicked out blindly, and all the other animals plunged with a sympathetic fear. Struggle was useless. An Aurigan was there; the figure of Death itself, with its unwearying scythe and unaltering smile of bone, was as easily avoided as this poisoned and unseen presence. A rosy flush spread over the back of one of the sows. Almost at once, her great bulk began to collapse; in a moment, her substance had been ingested.

Gregory did not stay to watch the sickening action. He was running forward, for the farmer was again on

the move. And now it was clear what he was going to do. He pushed into the end sty and dropped his daughter down into the metal food trough. At once, the sows turned with smacking jaws to deal with this new fodder. His hands free, Grendon moved to a bracket set in the wall. There lay his gun.

Now the uproar in the sties had reached its loudest. The sow whose companion had been so rapidly ingested broke free and burst into the central aisle. For a moment she stood—mercifully, for otherwise Gregory would have been trampled—as if dazed by the possibility of liberty. The place shook and the other swine fought to get to her. Brick crumbled, pen gates buckled. Gregory jumped aside as the second pig lumbered free, and next moment the place was full of grotesque fighting bodies, fighting their way to liberty.

He had reached Grendon, but the stampede caught them even as they confronted each other. A hoof stabbed down on Grendon's instep. Groaning, he bent forward, and was at once swept underfoot by his creatures. Gregory barely had time to vault into the nearest pen before they thundered by. Nancy was trying pitifully to climb out of the trough as the two beasts to which she had been offered fought to kick their way free. With a ferocious strength—without reason—almost without consciousness—Gregory hauled her up, jumped until he swung up on one of the overhead beams, wrapped a leg round the beam, hung down till he grasped Nancy, pulled her up with him.

They were safe, but the safety was not permanent. Through the din and dust, they could see that the gigantic beasts were wedged tightly in both entrances. In the middle was a sort of battlefield, where the animals fought to reach the opposite end of the building; they were gradually tearing each other to pieces—but the sties too were threatened with demolition.

"The Aurigan is here somewhere," Gregory shouted. "We aren't safe from it by any means."

"You were foolish to come here, Greg," Nancy said. "I found you had gone and I had to follow you. But Father—I don't think he even recognized me!"

At least, Gregory thought, she had not seen her father trampled underfoot. Involuntarily glancing in that direction, he saw the shotgun that Grendon had never managed to reach still lying across a bracket on the wall. By crawling along a transverse beam, he could reach it easily. Bidding Nancy sit where she was, he wriggled along the beam, only a foot or two above the heaving backs of the swine. At least the gun should afford them some protection: the Aurigan, despite all its ghastly differences from humanity, would hardly be immune to lead.

As he grasped the old-fashioned weapon and pulled it up, Gregory was suddenly filled with an intense desire to kill one of the invisible monsters. In that instant, he recalled an earlier hope he had had of them: that they might be superior beings, beings of wisdom and enlightened power, coming from a better society where higher moral codes directed the activities of its citizens. He had thought that only to such a civilization would the divine gift of travelling through interplanetary space be granted. But perhaps the opposite held true: perhaps such a great objective could be gained only by species ruthless enough to disregard more humane ends. As soon as he thought it, his mind was overpowered with a vast diseased vision of the universe, where such races as dealt in love and kindness and intellect cowered forever on their little globes, while all about them went the slayers of the universe, sailing where they would to satisfy their cruelties and their endless appetites.

He heaved his way back to Nancy above the bloody porcine fray.

She pointed mutely. At the far end, the entrance

had crumbled away, and the sows were bursting forth into the night. But one sow fell and turned crimson as it fell, sogging over the floor like a shapeless bag. Another, passing the same spot, suffered the same fate.

Was the Aurigan moved by anger? Had the pigs, in their blind charging, injured it? Gregory raised the gun and aimed. As he did so, he saw a faint hallucinatory column in the air; enough dirt and mud and blood had been thrown up to spot the Aurigan and render him partly visible. Gregory fired.

The recoil nearly knocked him off his perch. He shut his eyes, dazed by the noise, and was dimly aware of Nancy clinging to him, shouting, "Oh, you marvellous man, you marvellous man! You hit that old bor right smack on target!"

He opened his eyes and peered through the smoke and dust. The shade that represented the Aurigan was tottering. It fell. It fell among the distorted shapes of the two sows it had killed, and corrupt fluids splattered over the paving. Then it rose again. They saw its progress to the broken door, and then it had done.

For a minute they sat there, staring at each other, triumph and speculation mingling on both their faces. Apart from one badly injured beast, the building was clear of pigs now. Gregory climbed to the floor and helped Nancy down beside him. They skirted the loathsome masses as best they could and staggered into the fresh air.

Up beyond the orchard, strange lights showed in the rear windows of the farmhouse.

"It's on fire! Oh, Greg, our poor home is afire! Quick, we must gather what we can! All father's lovely cases—"

He held her fiercely, bent so that he spoke straight into her face. "Bert Neckland did this! He did it! He told me the place ought to be destroyed and that's what he did."

"Let's go, then—"

"No, no, Nancy, we must let it burn! Listen! There's a wounded Aurigan loose here somewhere. We didn't kill him. If those things feel rage, anger, spite, they'll be set to kill us now—don't forget there's more than one of 'em! We aren't going that way if we want to live. Daisy's just across the meadow here, and she'll bear us both safe home."

"Greg, dearest, this is my home!" she cried in her despair.

The flames were leaping higher. The kitchen window broke in a shower of glass. He was running with her in the opposite direction, shouting wildly, "I'm your home now! I'm your home now!"

Now she was running with him, no longer protesting, and they plunged together through the high rank grass.

When they gained the track and the restive mare, they paused to take breath and look back.

The house was well ablaze now. Clearly nothing could save it. Sparks had carried to the windmill, and one of the sails was ablaze. About the scene, the electric lights shone spectral and pale on the tops of their poles. An occasional running figure of a gigantic animal dived about its own purposes. Suddenly, there was a flash as of lightning and all the electric lights went out. One of the stampeding animals had knocked down a pole; crashing into the pond, it short-circuited the system.

"Let's get away," Gregory said, and he helped Nancy on to the mare. As he climbed up behind her, a roaring sound developed, grew in volume and altered in pitch. Abruptly it died again. A thick cloud of steam billowed above the pond. From it rose the space machine, rising, rising, rising, suddenly a sight to take the heart in awe. It moved up into the soft night sky, was lost for a moment, began dully to glow, was seen to be already tremendously far away.

Desperately, Gregory looked for it, but it had

gone, already beyond the frail confines of the terrestrial atmosphere. An awful desolation settled on him, the more awful for being irrational, and then he thought, and cried his thought aloud, "Perhaps they were only holiday-makers here! Perhaps they enjoyed themselves here, and will tell their friends of this little globe! Perhaps Earth has a future only as a resort for millions of the Aurigan kind!"

The church clock was striking midnight as they passed the first cottages of Cottersall.

"We'll go first to the inn," Gregory said. "I can't well disturb Mrs. Fenn at this late hour, but your landlord will fetch us food and hot water and see that your cuts are bandaged."

"I'm right as rain, love, but I'd be glad of your company."

"I warn you, you shall have too much of it from now on!"

The door of the inn was locked, but a light burned inside, and in a moment the landlord himself opened to them, all eager to hear a bit of gossip he could pass on to his customer.

"So happens as there's a gentleman up in Number Three wishes to speak with you in the morning," he told Gregory. "Very nice gentleman came on the night train, only got in here an hour past, off the waggon."

Gregory made a wry face.

"My father, no doubt."

"Oh, no sir. His name is a Mr. Wills or Wells—his signature was a mite difficult to make out."

"Wells! Mr. Wells! So he's come!" He caught Nancy's hands, shaking them in his excitement. "Nancy, one of the greatest men in England is here! There's no one more profitable for such a tale as ours! I'm going up to speak with him right away."

Kissing her lightly on the cheek, he hurried up the stairs and knocked on the door of Number Three.